Alan Hunter was born in Hoveton, Norfolk in 1922. He left school at the age of fourteen to work on his father's farm, spending his spare time sailing on the Norfolk Broads and writing nature notes for the *Eastern Evening News*. He also wrote poetry, some of which was published while he was in the RAF during the Second World War. By 1950, he was running his own bookshop in Norwich. In 1955, the first of what would become a series of forty-six George Gently novels was published. He died in 2005, aged eighty-two.

The Inspector George Gently series

Gently North-West

Alan Hunter

ROBINSON

Constable & Robinson Ltd
55–56 Russell Square
London WC1B 4HP
www.constablerobinson.com

First published in the UK by Cassell & Company Ltd, 1967

This paperback edition published by Robinson,
an imprint of Constable & Robinson Ltd, 2012

A copy of the British Library Cataloguing in
Publication Data is available from the British Library

ISBN: 978-1-78033-940-5 (paperback)
ISBN: 978-1-78033-941-2 (ebook)

Typeset by TW Typesetting, Plymouth, Devon

Printed and bound by CPI Group (UK) Ltd, Croydon, CR0 4YY

1 3 5 7 9 10 8 6 4 2

In memory of my mother, Isabella Hunter, née Andrews, formerly of Newton Lodge, Culsalmond, Aberdeenshire, who, in the short time permitted her, and among the flats and barbarians of East Norfolk, contrived to possess her son with an indelible prejudice for the land of heroes and poets. Rest her well where she lies, and greetings to my unknown Scottish cousins.

Norwich, 1966

Mr Fred Urquhart undertook the labour of vetting my Scots and vainly attempted to argue me out of three parts of it. I am to blame, he is scatheless. My best thanks are due to him for his generous endeavours.

A.H.

CHAPTER ONE

Pick up yer stick, Donald,
   Pu' on yer bonnet—
The North Road's a lang ane
   Wi' queer cattle on it.
         Later Border Minstrelsy, ed. McWheeble

T HE TWO CARS, both Humbers, one a blue Hawk *IV*, one a bronze-and-black Sceptre, approached Tally Ho Corner by Ballards Lane and there joined the Great North Road.

Like all good journeys, this one had begun very early in the morning. Bridget, Gently's sister, and her husband, Geoffrey Kelling, had arrived at Finchley from Somerset the evening before. Brenda Merryn had slept in Kensington, where she had a late surgery to take, but her green *1100* had slunk into Elphinstone Road shortly after 5.30 a.m. Gently, sprucely dressed in thorn-proof tweed, had answered her ring. He beheld Brenda elegant in a tailored suit and a discreet blouse with a ruffled front. She sent a look past Gently before she kissed him. She smelt like a bouquet of lilac.

'Are your sinister relatives about . . . ?'

'Naturally. They're going to eat you for breakfast.'

'I've told you before, George – you're a swine!'

Gently grinned and drew her into the hall.

Bridget and Geoffrey were already in the breakfast-room, which was warm with the odours of coffee and hot bacon. Bridget was very like her brother but she had grey eyes and her chin was less blunt. Geoffrey had a thin, ascetic face and surprisingly merry brown eyes. They both rose to take Brenda by the hand.

'My dear, you're not quite a stranger,' Bridget told her. 'We live only a few miles from Bristol, you know, and Geoff has met your father in court.'

'Yes,' Geoffrey nodded, 'to my utter confusion. He bowled over a respected client of mine. Taunton Assizes, '63. If you're a chip off old Eric I must watch my step.'

Gently winked at Bridget over Brenda's shoulder, but Bridget firmly avoided his eye.

Mrs Jarvis, wearing a flowered dressing-gown which Gently had given her at Easter, served the sort of breakfast which in her view was *de rigueur* for intending travellers to Scotland. Because it was so early there were no papers and no radio noises in the background, and the meal proceeded with gay briskness from porridge to toast and marmalade.

Gently, finishing first, went out to switch Brenda's luggage to the Sceptre; then he brought the Sceptre to the curb behind the Hawk and shunted the *1100* into the garage.

2

About him the morning air was cool. Slaty shadows lay along the road. And beyond that road was another road, and another road, and at last . . . Scotland! A whole fortnight of peaks and heather lay at the end of Elphinstone Road, waiting the twist of an ignition key, the surge of the Sceptre's sweet engine . . .

Gently glanced at his watch: 6.10. He could hear Brenda laughing in the house; and suddenly London felt like a prison from which he could scarcely wait to break free. With a fierce longing he wanted those mountains purpling in the rainy wrack, the flowery glens, the brabbling streams, the grey, wind-wrinkled lochs. Otterburn and the North! And Brenda to go by his side. Until that moment, standing by the cars, he hadn't guessed how much he wanted this trip.

Brenda came out of the house smiling and threw him a mock salute with two fingers.

'We're on time, O Highness,' she said. 'Take-off isn't till 6.15.'

'Being early won't hurt us,' Gently grumbled un-graciously. 'What's my sister forgotten this time?'

Bridget had forgotten her toilet-bag, as usual, and in fact they were two minutes late getting away.

Traffic was blissfully light when they first struck the A1. After Hatfield, they were drifting along at a steady, murmurous sixty-five, the Hawk leading, the Sceptre a precise thirty yards behind. Some early commuter traffic was meeting them but their own lane was thinly sown, and they were comfortably improving on the average which Gently had estimated in his travel-plan.

He drove relaxedly, his hands lying light on the wheel, his left thumb hooked in the perforated spoke, his right hand extended along the rim. When he made a straight-through change it was a wrist- and not an arm-movement and the revs swelled or levelled to an imperceptible take-up. The Sceptre had been serviced two days before and she was handling like silk. She'd also been polished, vacuumed and valeted, and had her tyres upped three p.s.i.

They cleared the Stevenage motorway and bored on towards Baldock. The sun was standing up on their right in the blue fire of a June sky. Early June had been wet, following a cold, late spring, but since the beginning of the week the weather had turned brilliant.

'Ah,' Brenda sighed. 'This is the life for a jaded receptionist.'

Gently smiled without turning his head. 'It'll rain when we get to Scotland,' he said.

'Not in my Scotland it won't,' Brenda said. 'It may rain in yours, but not in mine. There'll be sun on the bens and the glens. I crossed a gypsy's palm with silver.'

'There'll be mist, there'll be rain,' Gently said. 'Then the brightest sun of all. Then the longest and softest evening. Then the rain and the rain and the rain.'

'Hm,' Brenda said. 'Gently the Rain King. You're a romantic, that's your trouble. But I'm a realist, I dabble in magic. I've witched the weather and it shan't rain.'

They reached the limits at Baldock and Gently closed up on the slowing Hawk. A big transporter was hammering towards them, leaving a trail of smoke along the street. His eyes on this, Gently failed to notice a car

4

come shooting up in his mirror, and a moment later a dark blue Cortina cut across in front of him with squealing tyres. He hit the brakes. The polite Sceptre ducked and obeyed. Smoke, fumes and the thunder of the transporter broke over and around them. Through a grimy mist Gently saw the Cortina swing out past the Hawk and pull away, then they were through the blackest of the smoke and coasting into slightly dimmed Baldock.

'Well, the bloody swine!' Brenda exclaimed, her green eyes flashing. 'Did you ever see such an exhibition – and breaking the speed limit on top! Did you get his number, George?'

Gently shook his head. 'Too busy.'

'But you're not going to let him get away with it?'

'What do you suggest – that I chase him?'

'Yes – something!' Brenda stormed. 'Good Lord, he's a menace, he'll kill someone. And you, you're a policeman, George – it's up to you to do something!'

Gently cocked a grin at her. 'Cool down,' he said. 'I'm just a Whitehall copper on his holidays. If I went chasing every firebrand on the A1 I'd never make it to the Border.'

'But he might have smashed us.'

'Not him. He knew I'd reach for my anchors.'

'And he was breaking the speed limit.'

'Very naughty. I hope they catch him and sting him for it.

'Oh, oh,' Brenda cried. 'But you didn't see him, and I did. He had long red hair and a red beard, and he looked the most conceited man in the world.'

'He probably travels in hair-restorer,' Gently said. 'That would account for the chip on his shoulder.'

'He's a devil,' Brenda said. 'I think he's a bank-bandit. And you're just letting him slip through your fingers.'

She jerked a cigarette from a tin on the shelf, put the lighter to it and puffed smoke meanly. She glared at Gently. Gently winked, sent the Sceptre gliding through the lights after Geoffrey.

They strode on again northwards, by Biggleswade, Sandy, St Neots. Gently pointed out a lay-by where had occurred a vicious killing he had investigated. The victim, an R.A.F. warrant officer, had been brought there in a van; then his body had been cut to ribbons with Sten-gun fire to confuse identity and suggest a revenge motive.

'You know such nice people,' Brenda commented. 'You're such a status-making acquaintance. Did you catch the murderer?'

'No, he escaped. He was a Pole. His countrymen got him.'

'What did they do to him?'

'Oh, gassed him one night.'

'I see. What you'd call a happy ending.'

'It was an amusing case,' Gently said. 'There was a woman in it. She got strangled.'

Then on by Huntingdon and Alconbury, where the A1 took the line of Ermine Street, and by Stamford, Grantham and Newark, crossing the cantle-cutting Trent. Names were different, houses were different, with more of stone and less of brick; a drystone wall or a strange poster told of the miles they'd left behind.

London, the south, were slipping away, their soft grain and prim surface; and the north was coming down to meet them, ruder, franker, more elemental. Even the A1, the unchanging A1, uniform in surface, sign and traffic, choosing always the featureless line of country, couldn't quite conceal the tang of the North.

By 10.15 they'd arrived at the south end of the Doncaster Motorway, and here Gently's travel-plan allowed for a stop for coffee and petrol. The two cars pulled into the service station and parked with bumpers to the low parapet. Their crews tumbled out, stretching, sniffing, a little bemused by the quietness and non-movement.

'It's inside, I think,' Brenda said to Bridget. 'Did you notice that pig in the blue Cortina?'

'Bridgy wouldn't notice anything,' Geoffrey said. 'She's one of those lucky people who can sleep in cars.'

'Well,' Brenda said, '*you'd* have noticed him. He passed you in the speed limit at Baldock.'

'May have done, my dear,' Geoffrey smiled. 'But then, we were crawling through Baldock in any case.'

'Oh,' Brenda said. 'You're worse than George.' And she went off with her nose tilted, towing Bridget after her.

They met again in the station's large, comfortably fitted restaurant, which framed, with a range of huge windows, the sweeping view to the north-west. There, drinking your coffee, you apparently looked out into an animated industrial painting, in which the motorway, advancing from a roundabout in the foreground, led the eye to a majestic spoil-tip in the middle distance.

'Perfect Lowry,' Geoffrey apostrophized. 'Though he was using somebody else's palette. To see Ruskin justified like this is enough to make an artist hang himself.'

'Of course, Geoff's brought his paints along,' Bridget said. 'We'll see some Monarchs of the Glen à la Doyly John.'

'Well, there are deer at Strathtudlem,' Geoffrey said. 'At least, Maclaren swore there were when he offered me the cottage.'

'And you believed him,' Bridget said.

'Yes – he was sober enough at the time. And he vouches for wild-cats in Strathtudlem Forest, and a golden eagle if we're lucky.'

'Did he vouch for Red MacGregors?' Brenda asked.

'Red MacGregors?'

Brenda nodded. 'Who scour the roads in blue Cortinas – then sit down to coffee with their victims.'

She pointed along the line of booths, in one of which they were sitting. Above the back of the last of them they could see projecting a head of fiery red hair.

'That's your man, Superintendent,' she said to Gently. 'You'd better slip along and put the cuffs on him.'

'What makes you so certain it's him?' Gently asked.

'Intuition, O Highness. But I'm willing to check.'

She slid out of the booth and marched down the aisle to the booth occupied by the red hair. Attached to the wall near the booth was a vending machine and at this she paused, as though examining its wares. Then she turned to stare accusingly at the owner of the hair. Then she marched back and resumed her seat by Gently.

'Yes,' she said. 'That's him. Redbeard in person. He's up to some devil's work with papers and a notebook – most likely checking his score of probables.'

'Pooh,' Gently said. 'He's only a traveller getting his programme worked out.'

'If you say so. But I'll tell you one thing: he's as Scotch as Wullie Wallace. He's got one of those mighty and mournful faces they use on tins of shortbread, and a big agate pin stuck in his tie, and a tartan waistcoat with silver buttons.'

'Is that a crime?'

'I don't know. But I wouldn't want to meet him around Bannockburn. Are you going to run him in?'

Gently chuckled. 'Not my day for it,' he said.

'*I* think his name's MacLandru,' Brenda said. 'Or else he's the Son of Rob Roy.'

When they rose to go the Cortina-driver was still sitting in his booth. Outside Brenda spotted his car. It was a G.T. model, much stained with travel.

The motorway took them into West Riding and the long, long Yorkshire miles, with Boroughbridge apparently receding before them and Leeds for ever riding their flank. The Sceptre had taken over the lead and was thrusting ahead through plentiful traffic, slipping tall trucks, frisky caravans, transporters loaded with bright new cars. Gently's pipe hung dead in his mouth and his eyes were distant and dreamy. The pattern of traffic seemed always to unfold for him, move from him, give him road. Leeds was weathered at last and Boroughbridge erased from the signs. Ripon, Thirsk and

9

Northallerton ceased to offer invitation. Then they were passing Catterick Camp with its long ranks of khaki trucks, and pointing up the straight to the great divide of Scotch Corner.

Gently glanced at his watch as he slowed for the roundabout.

'Well?' Brenda asked.

'Good going. I think we'll press on to Brough for lunch.'

'I'm hungry now,' Brenda yawned. 'And when do we get to some scenery?'

'Stay with it,' Gently said. 'We'll perhaps have lunch and scenery together.'

He turned left onto the A66, checking that Geoffrey had turned behind him. At once the anonymity of the A1 was broken and they began climbing into hilly country. At Bowes they reached the 1000-foot contour and were still climbing across Bowes moor, with a great width of raw Pennine fells stretching beside and beyond them. They stopped short of Brough and lunched at a roadhouse at the highest point of the road. Photographs on the wall showed arctic-like snow scenes, taken when the roadhouse had been cut off in a recent winter. Behind them the moors peaked in Boldoo Hill, before them stretched to Bastifell, Tan Hill, Water Crag; while down the road which the legions had trod appeared the first blue promise of the lakeland mountains.

'Oh,' Bridget exclaimed, as they stood in the car-park and took photographs like other tourists, 'why go any farther than this — what can Scotland have to beat it?'

'It's certainly a stunner,' Geoffrey agreed. 'I don't know — what's Scotland got, George?'

'Scotland is bigger,' Gently said. 'That's the important point about Scotland.'

'Oh, nonsense,' Geoffrey said. 'What can being bigger have to do with it?'

Gently shrugged. 'Just about everything. It's big enough to lose people.'

He pointed to the traffic streaming past, the belching trucks, the shouldering cars, their hot tyres pounding, pounding, pounding the Romans' road across the Pennines. Even to cross that road to the drystone wall was an enterprise of moment. Though the wall made the best vantage for the photographers, few were bothering to exploit it.

'Yes,' Brenda said, 'I understand, George. Getting lost is what counts.'

'George can say what he likes,' Bridget said. 'But he's about the last person to get lost, anywhere.'

They drove on, by Brough, by Appleby, making the lake mountains climb higher, then turning their back on them at Penrith to join the fast carriageways of the A6. The Hawk was leading again now and Brenda had taken the wheel of the Sceptre. She drove with a flair that contrasted with Gently's smooth discipline, which combined police coaching with natural poise and temperament.

They crept through rusty-faced Carlisle and bore left on the A74. Still it was England, though the classic boundary of the Wall lay behind them.

'Oh Highness,' Brenda sighed. 'This Scotland is certainly a far country. I've a feeling that if we go this way much longer we'll drive clean out at the top.'

11

'Just a little farther,' Gently said. 'We cross the Border at Gretna Green.'

Brenda threw him a glance. 'You kept that dark. If I'd known, you might have whistled for your Strathtudlem.'

'Just drive,' Gently said. 'Keep your mind on the job.'

'Yes, but it's difficult,' Brenda said. 'Driving a man like you through a place like that.'

And she whistled a few bars of 'Bonny Dundee', lilting her head in time with it.

'I suppose,' Gently said, from the depths of his pipe, 'on balance, your whiskery friend isn't a traveller.'

'Redbeard?' Brenda said, surprised. 'Have you been turning the trained mind on him?'

'Force of habit,' Gently grinned. 'He's the only likely material we've seen today. And now I consider it I'm inclined to agree with you. On balance, I don't think he's a traveller.'

'Well, one up to my intuition,' Brenda said. 'Why don't you think he's a traveller?'

'The car. It's not the model a traveller would use, nor a model a firm would supply to its reps.'

'A-hah,' Brenda said. 'But suppose he was in the car trade. Car-trade men often go for a hot car.'

'Yes, but they can usually drive them, too,' Gently said. 'And Redbeard's driving didn't impress us. No, on balance we can eliminate travellers. Also, I wouldn't place him in a profession. Professional men are required to conform in matters of dress and hairstyle.'

'A musician perhaps.'

'A musician is possible. But there again the car is unlikely.'

'Why?'

'Musicians are pariahs to insurers. He'd hardly get cover for a hot car.'

'Hm,' Brenda said. 'You're making it difficult. On balance, he soon isn't going to exist. But there he was with his beard and buttons, singeing the tyres of his G.T. So who does the trained mind say he was?'

Gently puffed. 'Could have been a farmer.'

'Oh, no. Never a farmer!'

'Why not? It fits most of the facts.' He counted on his fingers. 'One, a dirty car, with plenty of mud in the wheel arches. Two, a man who dresses flamboyantly and can't be bothered with razors and barbers. Three, a man who drives impatiently as though he's used to owning the road. Four, a man who employs a break in a journey to tot up figures in a notebook. Five, a man who uses a hot car but is satisfied with one of the cheapest. Add it up.'

'I won't,' Brenda said. 'You shan't make my Redbeard into a farmer.'

'I'd say he was in cattle,' Gently said. 'He's just been south with a shipment of bullocks.'

'He's a bank-robber at the least!'

'Probably from the Highlands,' Gently said. 'Your description of his features suggests that. Yes, a Highland farmer on his way home from a livestock sale.'

Brenda flickered him a venomous look. 'You're just rotten to me, aren't you, George?' she said. 'You know I can't stand up for myself, and you're brutal to me all the time.'

'It's my job,' Gently said. 'I'm a brutal policeman.'

'Well you are,' Brenda said. 'That's you all over. I'll bet you oil your thumbscrews every morning and blanco the webbing on your rack. Do you want to know something, George Gently?'

'Tell me,' Gently said.

'We've just passed through Gretna Green – and I wouldn't go back there if you paid me.'

And the tall sun, which had begun the day riding low on their right, was now standing to their left; and still the cars raced northwards. Eight spinning wheels turning, tilting the great globe itself, while the great globe itself revolved shining in its spaceway. But the drivers were growing tired now and speed was slowing with them, so that tyres occasionally scrubbed on a bend which arrived too fast; and eyes were wearying of impressions and seeing increasing sameness in every vista, with only enough of strangeness to make the fresh scene unfriendly. So the A74 became the A73, brushing Glasgow's wide urbation and crossing the big east-west arteries; reached Cumbernauld, took another bite north as the A80, then skirted Bannockburn to lose itself in the anonymous streets of Stirling. They crossed the Forth, but at this end of the day the Forth was just another river; came to Balmagussie, its broad street closed to the west by some bald-browed ben; drove now slower, because the twisted road was squeezed between loch and jealous braeside, the last, longest, weariest miles to the glen village of Strathtudlem.

And there the wheels stopped spinning, by the low white walls of Maclaren's cottage, the target of all those stretching roads from the Victorian villa in Finchley. And in the buzzing stillness a Scots voice was saying:

'My guidness! From London this morning, did ye say? But you'll be wanting your supper, that's certain. Step in – step in. And you from London!'

CHAPTER TWO

I went wi' Maggie up the glen,
 Donsie, sonsie Maggie Mackay;
When think ye we cam doun again?
 Whist! I mauna lie.
                'The Gauger's Wooing', attrib. Burns

AND YOU FROM London . . .! Perhaps no greeting
could have been more salutary, Gently thought. At
one stroke it turned them about from facing north to
facing south. London, till then, had travelled with them
like an aura they could not lose, but now suddenly a
cord had snapped and London vanished below the
horizon. They were in Scotland. The Town of Cockney
from here was merely another town; distinguished by
being distant, like Plymouth or Bristol, but not
otherwise greatly remarkable.

'You'll be Mrs McFie?' Geoffrey was saying to the
plump, smiling woman who showed them into the
cottage.

'Ay, and you'll be Mr Kelling, I don't doubt, who sees
to the Major's law-work in England. How is the Major?'

'Maclaren's well.'

'I had a letter from him on Tuesday. I'm to treat you like himself, the Major says, but no' to plague you with tup's head or haggis.'

'Oh,' Geoffrey said. 'What would tup's head be?'

'If ye dinna ken, Mr Kelling, you'll perhaps be better off without it.'

Maclaren's cottage made no pretension to being grander than its name suggested. One stepped straight from the porch into a low-ceilinged living-room littered with old and shabby furniture. The flagged floor was overlaid with mats and the rough walls were simply whitewashed, and so massively thick that the small window seemed to be set in a tunnel. A Welsh dresser, weighty with crockery, occupied much of the back wall, and a case of books, mainly fiction and sporting, was arranged to conceal a door into another room. By the window stood a large, solid table, covered and laid for four people. Perhaps because the walls were so ponderous the room had an air of great silence.

Mrs McFie, having made their acquaintance, retired to the kitchen to brew tea; but since the kitchen was next door to the living-room the remove was small bar to her conversation. From the kitchen also they soon began to hear a suggestive sizzle of hot fat, and a rich smell of frying started to percolate through the cottage.

Gently was feeling bone-tired. He had not driven so far for many a summer, and now he was glad to sprawl on a board-hard couch and sip a mighty cup of strong, sweet tea. Geoffrey, he noticed with some surprise, seemed quite unmarked by the trip. He was spryly hauling in luggage from the Hawk and keeping up a running chat with Mrs McFie. Brenda and Bridget, lugging travel-bags, had vanished into a scullery-cum-bathroom, but this too was so closely adjacent that one heard their voices and the sound of running water.

The cottage, Gently noticed, had a distinctive smell, over and above the smell of frying, a cold, church-like odour and faint seediness, yet with no suggestion of damp. On the living-room walls hung framed texts and one print after Landseer.

'Did Maclaren farm up this way, then?' Geoffrey asked, dumping the last of his cases and looking round for his tea.

'Oh ay, the Maclarens are an auld family up this way,' Mrs McFie's hot face said, poking round the doorway. 'The Major and his faither before him, and his grandfaither – auld Shoggie Maclaren – but the Forestry came here, ye ken, and they got in the Major's bad buiks over the hill pastures. So the Major ups and sells to Donald Dunglassall except this bit cottage – and takes himself off into England. He's a man of speerit, is the Major.'

'I'll second that,' Geoffrey grinned at Gently. 'He's the most obstinate and litigious Scotsman who ever set foot over the border.'

'Ay,' Mrs McFie's face assented, 'he's a one for the law, no doubt. I ken the time he's had five suits together goin' in to the sessions at Balmagussie. But Donald Dunglass, he's another fish – he's from Glesca, ye ken, not a proper farmer – but he wedded a McGuigan from Cuitybraggan. How will you have your tatties, Mr Kelling?'

The ladies returned looking sprucer, and supper was on the table soon after. It consisted of lamb chops, kidney, liver, fried sliced potatoes and fried oatmeal, or skurly. And strangely, Gently's appetite, which had been nil when he'd sat down on the couch, was now man enough to deal with these items and the pancakes and honey and jam that followed. Slowly, the journey was easing out of him and being replaced by the cool silence of the cottage. He ate without joining in the conversation, but gazing out of the small deep window opposite him. When he lit his pipe he caught Brenda watching him.

'So,' she said. 'What's the great man staring at?'

Gently smiled. 'Just that bit of a peak. I'm going to be neighbours with it for a fortnight.'

'So,' Brenda said.

'So it's there. And if we're going to live with it, we'll have to climb it.'

'Oh will we then,' Brenda said, peering through the window. 'It looks a pretty hairy prospect to me. You'll perhaps manage the bit through the trees all right, but you'll soon get stuck when it turns craggy. And even where the trees are it looks sheer. Aren't I right, Mrs McFie?'

'Ay,' said Mrs McFie, coming in that moment to collect the plates. 'There's a guid Forestry path up to the Keekingstane, but it's only for sheep after that.'

'You see?' Brenda said. 'I'm always right. What's the Keekingstane, Mrs McFie?'

'Just that queer rock at the top of the craig – a look-out, ye ken, in the aulden times. They could put

19

a man on the stane and he could keek at what was coming up the glen – they were a terrible lot in those days, aye fightin' and murderin' each other.'

'And there's a good path to it?' Gently asked.

'Guid enough when it's dry. Ye'll find a gate just across the bridge, with a Forestry notice beside it.'

'What do they call the hill?'

Mrs McFie laughed. 'Ye'll no' pull my leg, now, if I tell ye? In Strathtudlem we call it the Hill of the Fairies – though ye wouldna find the name on a map.'

'The Hill of the Fairies,' Brenda said. 'That's lovely . . . yes, it really is.'

'Well, you won't get me up there,' Geoffrey said. 'Not to meet the Queen of the Fairies in person.'

Mrs MacFie washed-up and bustled away, promising to be in early to cook their breakfast. Though apparently she lived only two doors off she put on a coat for the expedition, and drew a black, bonnet-like hat over her crimped and dyed locks. She turned to give them a last smile as she hastened by the little window.

'And that's us,' Brenda said. 'Oh, if I had that woman in Kensington! But some millionaire would pinch her if I did. He'd offer her mink, or just marry her.'

'Well, you don't know about her cooking,' Bridget said. 'You can't judge it on the basis of one Scotch high tea.'

'What's wrong with Scotch high teas at every meal,' Brenda said. 'Why not always eat food? They seem to thrive on it up here.'

Gently said: 'How about a stroll to help the one Scotch high tea settle?'

'And a dram at the local,' Geoffrey said. 'Who knows what the Scots drink among themselves?'

Though it was 9 p.m., the strangely suspended Highland evening was still brilliant in the glen, with sun pouring over the mountains to the west to flood the tops of those to the east. The glen was perhaps fifteen miles long and in the shape of a flattened S, so that its steep sides, shaggy with conifers, appeared to fold in on each other in both directions. A broad river flowed through it to join the loch at the southern end, and formed the strath, or alluvial flats, by which the village was built. The strath was meadowland. To the west of the road, where the only buildings were a shop and a garage, extended flowery meadows, intersected by the river, to the edge of the forest that fledged the braes. The houses facing these on the east had doubtless been sited for firm foundation. They made a line of brick and whitewashed fronts separated from the road by rough stone paving. The largest building, the Bonnie Strathtudlem, was late Victorian stone-quoined brick; and few of the other dwellings, with their slate or sheet-iron roofs, seemed likely to post-date it. Directly opposite the village the Hill of the Fairies lifted its blunt peak of grey, rose-tinted rock, and established a separate identity from the braes with a treeless blaze of broken crag.

The two men and two women loitered down the road towards the inn. The satiety of travel had left them now and they felt buoyed and absorbed by the scene about them. The air was soft yet exhilarating and miraculously clear, allowing minute detail of the sunlit tops and ten thousand trees to show vividly. It carried a faint odour of wild chervil, which here still flowered in the meadows, and in its hush one could hear the murmuring of the river from behind a screen of ash and alder.

As they neared the Bonnie Strathtudlem they became aware of other sounds.

'The devils, they're having a Gaelic hop!' Geoffrey exclaimed. 'Listen, that lad with the accordion is no fool.'

'Ought we to go in there, Geoff?' Bridget asked. 'It's probably a private affair. We should look foolish if they asked us to make a set in a strathspey.'

'Oh nonsense,' Geoffrey said. 'Probably do us good after a day in the car. Anyway, I'm game – what do you say, George?'

Gently laughed. 'I could probably tap my feet a little,' he said. 'But I'd sooner stroll down that lane and take a look at the river.'

So they passed the Bonnie Strathtudlem, before which a dozen cars were parked, and turned left to a narrow stone bridge which carried a minor road across the river. The river was fast-running and transparent, and made deep pools near the bridge. Staring into the pools it seemed imposible one should miss seeing a salmon or a monster trout. There the water appeared so still, while a yard away it was rushing and white; and under the bridge it positively thundered as it swooped down some concealed declivity.

'The fishing's free,' Geoffrey said, in the indifferent tone of a non-angler. 'You can hire rods at the inn, Maclaren says. Plenty of trout, or whatever you go for.'

'Trout will do,' Gently said.

'Well, it's apparently a good spot. Maclaren comes up here for the fishing, that's why he keeps the cottage on.'

'My respects to Maclaren,' Gently said. 'I begin to admire that man very much.'

The midges buzzed and brushed at their faces, and Geoffrey turned again towards the Bonnie Strathtudlem. The siren strain of the Bluebell Polka was now sounding from that direction. But Gently, casting an eye up the road, had spotted the gate mentioned by Mrs McFie, and wanted at least to view the point of departure of the 'guid path' to the Keekingstane.

'Oh come now, George,' Geoffrey objected. 'We all know where listening to you will get us. It'll just be one thing after another till we're at the top of that blessed mountain.'

'Maybe a few steps up it,' Gently grinned. 'Just to the first place with a view.'

'Yes, and up to our knees in bogs before we've gone a dozen yards!'

In the end they separated, with Brenda electing to accompany Gently. If they were not down by closing-time, Geoffrey said, he'd alert Whitehall and the Mountain Rescue.

The road over the bridge formed a T-junction with a narrow back-road behind the strath, and almost opposite the junction was the wooden field gate with its bright Forestry notice. The notice informed the public of its privilege to use, but not abuse, the Forestry tracks, but offered no indication of where the track was supposed

23

to be. In effect the gate opened into a grassy tangle of small bushes, broken by rock outcrop and shaded by tall oaks and graceful ashes. To the right a noisy torrent burled down over green, gloomy boulders, and some way off, on the strath side of the road, a large house showed through the trees. Brenda nodded towards the house.

'We could ask the laird. He should know where the track is.'

'I think it's towards the left,' Gently said. 'The other way we'd run into that torrent.'

'If Highness says so. But I'd love to meet a real heather-bashing laird.'

'They went out with hansom cabs,' Gently said. 'Come on. This is the only way that makes sense.'

He led through a thin curtain of underbrush into a grassy space divided by a rivulet, and here a couple of stones which might have been stepping-stones suggested that others used that way. A diagonal line across the opening brought them to a plantation of young firs, where a definite path upward was indicated by a lane or fire-break through the trees. It was rocky and muddy and obstructed with brush and quite unnecessarily perpendicular, and seemed to be going on for ever with no other prospect but more trees.

'Do you think it's right?' Brenda gasped at last. 'You owe me a new pair of shoes already.'

'It's right,' Gently grunted. 'There's someone ahead of us. We keep passing fresh bootmarks and snapped twigs.'

'Oh hell,' Brenda panted. 'These bloody professionals. I'll tell you something about him too.'

'What's that?'

'He's no stupid English tourist. He's a native who knows about "guid paths"!'

But at last the fire-break came to an end and plunged them into the twilight of some matured firs, beneath which the bare soil, slippery with needles, made them grab for handholds as they clambered upwards. Then there was day-light again. They had reached the lowest of the horizontal breaks, a broad, grassed, friendly-looking strip carrying a fence of sheep-netting. There was a gate in the fence and beside the gate a smooth stone. Brenda plumped down on the stone and gasped and dashed the hair from her eyes.

'This stone is the first sign I've met that the Forestry is human!'

Gently hung himself on the gate, taking great lungfuls of earthy air. In a way the break was disappointing, because it suggested a view it didn't offer. It curved at each end into the sky, just refusing a glimpse of the glen, while below and above them were merely trees and more trees.

'We're not so fit,' he puffed. 'Or maybe just not used to mountains.'

'Do you like your women sweaty?' Brenda gasped. 'Oh, why didn't I listen to Geoffrey? I *like* Geoffrey.'

'We're high, I think. We can't be far from the foot of the crag.'

'George, you can *keep* the crag.'

'Look, more bootmarks.'

'Oh!' Brenda panted. 'Oh!'

After ten minutes the sweat began drying and they'd

got their second wind; then another push at the track seemed a little less daunting. Beyond the gate it looked docile. Gently was convinced it would soon turn left towards the crag, and Brenda remembered seeing, when down at the cottage, a slanting ridge which could have been the path. So they went through the gate and on upwards, though with not quite the *élan* of the first onset. Now, after each hundred yards or so, they paused to breathe and wipe sweat.

The track indeed turned left: but only after another punishing ascent, followed by a scramble under young firs planted so thickly that beneath them was almost total blackness. Then it bore away in a steep, broken, slippery traverse, pointing to a goal of increased daylight above the dark night of the trees.

'That'll be it,' Gently gulped. 'There's a big gap up there.'

'Alleluia,' Brenda moaned. 'I'm not the girl I used to be. My poor, poor shoes.'

'I'll buy you some more in Balmagussie.'

'If you don't you're a rotten swine – and you're a rotten swine anyway.'

The end came suddenly. At one moment they were dragging themselves over the rocks, with trees hemming them on both sides and threatening to bar the way ahead; the next they were out on soft turf, in a nakedness of light that dazzled them, with a soaring rockface on one hand and airy nothing on the other. They had reached the crag. At its foot was no more than a shallow apron of grass, ending in a second precipice and a rockfall which were hidden from below by the trees.

They stood gasping, looking.

'Worth it now?' Gently asked.

Brenda shook her head. 'Nothing's worth it – but it's a pretty good view.'

'That's the cottage.'

'So what about it?'

'Those are the cars.'

'I've seen a car.'

'Look at the sun on the tops over there.'

'George.'

'Yes?'

'Drop dead,' Brenda said.

She slumped down on the turf and lay flapping at her face with her hand. Gently grinned at her through his sweat and threw himself down beside her.

The view was majestic. At this elevation the eastern braes had lost their steepness, and showed rolling heathy tops above the line of the forest. Southward the run of the glen was visible to its portal seven miles off, where, terminated on the right by a massive peak, it appeared to launch into the sky. All the loch could be seen. Its slanty reaches lay pale and skylike among the braes, at this end broad, with rushy boundaries, then narrowing to a distant silver arrow. Northward, where a secondary glen came in from the west, the strath broadened to a small plain, and the folding braes grouped around it to form a cauldron of misty woods.

They lay silently watching for several minutes, then Brenda turned to Gently with a smile.

'Big enough for you?'

He took her hand. 'Yes, big enough. Just.'

'Of course you're right about the size.'

'Yes.'

'It's what really makes the difference. With men too, as well as mountains. Do you think Bridget likes me?'

'Bridget likes you.'

'It's important.'

'Everything's important and unimportant.'

'Well, this is important.'

'Bridget likes you.'

'I could, of course, kick your teeth in.'

Gently kissed her.

'I wonder,' she said, 'if I could make you jealous, George. You're so damned impregnable, that's your trouble. Even if you were jealous it wouldn't show.'

'So why bother,' Gently said.

'Just an urge. All women have it. To make a man seething mad. To make it eat into his guts.'

'Well, don't frustrate the urge,' Gently said.

'But what's the use if you don't react?'

'I might pretend, to help out.'

'Jump over that cliff,' she said.

He kissed her.

Brenda gave a little wriggle in his arms. 'On the whole you talk too much,' she said. 'Not, in the normal way, that you talk a lot, but George, you do talk too much. Now please be quiet.'

'Yes,' Gently said.

'Quieter still.'

Gently was quiet.

'Even quieter.'

Gently obeyed.

'There,' she said. 'Much better.'

Gently was quiet then for a space of minutes; but now the sun on the tops was plainly waning. Soon even their lavish Highland evening would be stealing into a night. The dagger of the loch had grown harder, whiter in its thrust down the glen, and a haze was settling in the witch's pot and dulling the clean lines of the braes.

'Damn these mountains,' Brenda sighed. 'They're damp too, into the bargain.'

'Up then,' Gently said. 'When you notice that, it's time to go.'

He helped her rise. For a few last moments they dallied to take a farewell look, Brenda resting on Gently's arm with a hand curled inside his. Behind them the crag, splintered and fissured, lifted in dizzying pitches to the Keekingstane, and on the right the 'guid path' departed untamed into a fresh torment of trees. Suddenly Gently felt Brenda go taut.

'What is it?' he asked.

'Ssh. Just look.'

'Look where?'

'There. Up the crag. Then get ready to tell me I'm a liar.'

Gently looked. The crag rose perpendicularly for perhaps another two hundred feet, ending in a cloven shaft or tooth of rock which could be no other than the Stane. The Stane leaned outwards from the line of the crag and was silhouetted by the paling sky. In the cleft of the Stane Gently saw a man's head. The man was staring intently through a pair of glasses.

'I see,' Gently breathed. 'That explains all the boot-prints.'

'Don't you see who it is?' Brenda whispered.

'No. Nor do you at this distance.'

'But I do!' she hissed. 'I'd know him anywhere. I know the shape of his head.'

'Whose?'

'Redbeard's.'

'Dear Brenda!'

'Look,' she said. 'He's lowering the glasses.'

The glasses sank, and very briefly they glimpsed a broad, bearded face; then the man apparently caught sight of them and his head vanished from the cleft.

'There,' Brenda said. 'Now call me a liar!'

Gently hunched a shoulder. 'It's him if you say so. Maybe I was wrong about him being a farmer. Maybe he's a Forestry man instead.'

'Do Forestry men sit around with glasses?'

'He could be the laird from the big house. He was training the glasses in that direction.'

'A laird,' Brenda said. 'Yes, that's more like it.'

She gazed back interestedly up the crag, but the laird, if he was one, failed to oblige. Only the chill evening sky showed emptily through the cleft.

Brenda shivered.

'Let's go,' she said. 'He's probably on his way down.'

'Don't you want to meet him?'

'Some other time. Right now I'll settle for that dram at the local.'

CHAPTER THREE

Then the justicing-man wi' his fule bodies
  Cam' gawkin at Willie like a wheen auld hoodies.
    'Willie loupit o'er a linn', Lady Coupar

WHEN GENTLY WOKE in the morning a grey twilight was pervading his room and a low susurrous buzzing sounded continuously in his ears. He stirred uneasily. Could the Bonnie Strathtudlem's whisky really be so potent? But no, he'd only had time for a single tot, and apart from the buzzing his head felt clear enough. What, then . . . ?

The hissing wheels of a passing vehicle explained the matter. It was raining out there – Highland rain, which sends down three drops for one of any other sort.

He rolled out of bed and padded to the window. Yes, it was whirring down like a new Flood. The braes were sheeted in smoky wrack and the Hill of the Fairies was lost to view. Just outside the window the gleaming Hawk had spray dancing frolics on its roof, and each fresh car that swished by travelled in a screen-high

31

swathe of water. Highland rain! Why was it inspiriting, when London rain only depressed?

He found Geoffrey in a dressing-gown in the kitchen, drinking tea with Mrs McFie. Mrs McFie was stirring porridge in a black iron saucepan. Both were looking rather solemn, Geoffrey through the window at the rain, Mrs McFie at the porridge, which bubbled fatly as she stirred.

'Ay, is it you?' she said when Gently entered. 'I canna wish ye a very quid mornin'. As I've been tellin' Mr Geoffrey, we talked it up – we talked it up.'

'Oh I don't know,' Gently said, looking round for the tea-pot. 'It's much about what I expected. You're never dry for long in these parts.'

'It's no' the rain, Mr Gently,' Mrs McFie said tartly. 'What goes up must come down, there's no goin' against that. No, it's just us talkin' of the Hill in a fliskish sort o' way – it doesna do. There's ay some trouble for idle folk to talk up.'

'We've offended the wee folk,' Geoffrey said. 'Seems there's been an accident, George.'

'Oh,' Gently said, pouring tea. 'Sorry to hear it. I hope nobody was hurt.'

'That's very likely,' Mrs McFie said. 'Wi' half the polis from Balmagussie out here – an' an ambulance, what's more – an' the Inspector laddie in plain clothes. No, no, they wouldna be shankin' around up there for just nothin'. They're thick as fleas up the paths – they'll find it more damp than dry, I'm thinkin'.'

'Up the paths,' Gently said, staring. 'What paths are those, Mrs McFie?'

'Why the Forestry paths, what else? It's up at the Stane McMorris found him.'

'Hrrumph! Hrrumph!' Geoffrey coughed. 'Judges' Rules, George, Judges' Rules. As Mrs McFie is pointing out, the accident happened up the path we were asking about last night. Coincidence, what?'

Gently said nothing.

'It's not a coincidence,' Mrs McFie said. 'There's such a thing as talkin' up trouble, and ye winna persuade me out o' that.'

Gently poured and stirred tea and took a long, scalding sip. He glanced at Geoffrey; Geoffrey nodded delicately and gave a judicial flick of the eyebrow.

'Mrs McFie,' he said. 'Are you sure it's this Mr Dunglass who's met with an accident?'

'Ay,' Mrs McFie said. 'And how should I not be sure, when I had it from my ain cousin?'

'Your own cousin?'

'Ay, Johnny Dalgirdy, that's been gardener at the Lodge since the Major's time. He lives in the wee bit cottage across the road – my mother's uncle's wife was a Maisie Dalgirdy.'

'And when did the accident happen?'

'Ye may weel ask that, Mr Kelling. Donald Dunglass went off in his car last night and says he's away to Balmagussie.'

'But he was found by the Stane.'

'Ay. McMorris found him – that's Andy McMorris, the Forestry man. He was goin' his round of the fences, ye ken – I daresay that would be early on.'

'But what would Dunglass be doing up there?'

33

Mrs McFie wagged her gingery tresses. 'No doubt the polis are askin' that question, but Johnny didna ken the answer. Of course, Donald Dunglass owns the braeside – lock and stock, down to Halfstarvit – it's all lease-work wi' the Forestry, though ye canna exactly say them nay – but what he'd be doin' up there after dark is something ye maun ask Donnie.'

'Have they found his car?'

'I dinna ken that.'

'Do you know the make?'

'Ay – American. One of those over-risen sort of vehicles, like a patty-pan wi' four wheels.'

Tim,' Geoffrey said. 'This Donald Dunglass. I know a Dunglass at my club. He'd be a big, broad-shouldered type, would he – red hair, and a beard?'

'Nothin' o' that sort,' Mrs McFie said. 'He's just a Glesca body, is Donald Dunglass. No but the average run, ye ken, and I doubt if his chin would manage a beard.'

'I'm perhaps confusing him with someone else,' Geoffrey said. 'But I'm certain my man comes from these parts. Does his description suggest anyone to you?'

'Ay,' Mrs McFie said. 'Robert the Bruce.'

Breakfast was a sombre, thoughtful meal, despite Mrs McFie's real oatmeal porridge. The rain kept tumbling down outside and the wrack drifted steadily over the braes. An occasional figure, clutching its sack or groundsheet, plunged with bended head past their window, and among the few cars that planed by Gently recognized a police Super Snipe. For what were they searching out there, up the hill paths and under the mist?

34

A queer accident it needed to be to make an effort on this scale necessary.

At last Mrs McFie adjusted her defences and departed into the storm, and they were able for the first time to talk freely of the situation.

'George,' Bridget said. 'If you land us in this I'll never go on holiday with you again. It isn't necessary, and you're not to do it – there are plenty of policemen here to handle things.'

'It's a nice point,' Geoffrey said. 'But I think I'd advise the same thing. To our best information there has been only an accident, and you don't know that your friend Redbeard was concerned in it. You've seen him before, you saw him up there, that's the extent of your testimony. He could say exactly the same of you. There are no grounds to suppose his being there is particularly significant.'

'It isn't an accident,' Gently said.

'Ça va,' Geoffrey said. 'I bow to your judgement. But the argument holds, you know no evil of him. Therefore, volunteer nothing. The local police have tongues in their heads.'

'That's just what I say,' Bridget said. 'If they want information about this man they'll jolly soon come asking. And anyway, you don't know they don't know about him.'

'That again,' Geoffrey said. 'He may be talking to them at this moment George – about a courting couple up from London.'

Gently looked at Brenda. 'What do you say?'

Brenda tilted her chin and mouthed cigarette smoke.

35

'I say I do know evil of him,' she said. 'I put him down for a crook the moment I saw him.'

'Ah, but that's just opinion,' Geoffrey said.

'I'm good at opinions,' Brenda said. 'The first time I was ever one of George's suspects I formed the opinion I was going to like him. And Redbeard is evil. I could feel it last night. He wasn't playing peekaboo up there with his glasses. He was up to something nasty – and something nasty has happened. I'll bet they'll find out he did it, in the end.'

'Yes, but that isn't going to help the police,' Geoffrey said.

'The police are stupid. They should always listen to one of my intuitions.'

'Do you want to go to them, then?'

'No. I've another intuition about that. If George sticks his nose in over there they'll simply grab him with both hands.'

'Yes, probably as a suspect,' Gently grunted. 'Time, place, opportunity.'

'Well, you should know,' Geoffrey chuckled. 'Your reactions are the same as theirs.'

Gently stared gloomily at the rain, the oozing strath, the rolling vapour.

'Yes,' he said. 'That's the whole trouble. My reactions are the same as theirs. I know how they feel out there, especially if they're getting nowhere, and me sitting here with perhaps just the lead that'll make all their pieces fall into place. It's happened to me too many times, being stuck because someone refused to come forward. I'd like to say Hang you Jack with the rest, but it sticks in my throat; I know what's involved. Can you guess what they're looking for up the braes?'

Geoffrey's thick brows bunched. 'Could be a weapon.'

'A weapon – which may or may not be there. And for which they could be searching from now till Christmas.'

'And you think you can find it for them?' Bridget asked sourly.

'I might be able to suggest a better place to start looking.'

'Which would make you instantly popular with a lot of wet policemen.'

'Wet policemen are as miserable as wet civilians.'

'Yes, well,' Geoffrey frowned. 'I do see your point, of course, George. The pity of it is we don't know enough to know if your information is valuable or not. I still suggest you play it canny and wait to see how things develop. There's no need to put your foot in the bath till you see the colour of the water.'

'What a horrid metaphor,' Brenda said. 'It suggests bog-water soupy with peat.'

'But you agree with me, Brenda,' Geoffrey smiled.

'I did till the metaphor. Now I don't.'

'We're back every time to knowing too little, though I daresay Mrs McFie will soon remedy that. But till she does my advice is caution. We can always respond when we get a cue.'

'I see,' Brenda said. 'Our lawyer's advice. It only remains now for us to ignore it.'

'You won't do that?'

'If I don't, George will. Surely you know better than to offer him advice.'

'Ah,' Geoffrey said. He looked at Gently.

Slowly Gently nodded his head. 'Sorry, Geoffrey,' he said. 'Sorry, Bridget. But I'll just be a bear until I've talked to them. Brenda can stay out of it.'

'No fear,' Brenda said. 'Where you go, I go.'

'It shouldn't take long. And there's no danger of Scottish police trying to co-opt me on to their case.'

'That I'll believe when I hear it,' Bridget said. 'And Brenda had far better let you go on your own.'

'Ah me, but I'm a sucker for punishment,' Brenda said. 'Come on, George. Duty to death.'

With windscreen-wipers thrashing busily the Sceptre sluiced along the village street, turned left to cross the bridge, then right to Strathtudlem Lodge. At the gate to the track a constable was stationed, a dark, dripping, hunching figure, his raincoat supplemented by a cloak and a plastic cover over his chequered peak-cap.

'Accident!' Gently grunted, nodding at him. 'Who do they think they're kidding with that tale?'

'Poor boy. I can feel the water trickling down his back.'

'Likely enough he was off-duty when they grabbed him for this job.'

They drove through the Lodge gate and up a carriage-way of granite chippings. Three police cars were parked outside the house and a second constable guarded the porch. The Lodge was a tall, white-plastered house with clustering small gables and dormers; it had stone-framed and mullioned windows at ground-floor level and a pargetted crest above the porch.

'The laird's house,' Brenda whispered. 'We did get to visiting it after all.'

Gently 'humphed' – and parked the Sceptre as near the steps of the porch as it would go.

The constable came hastily down the steps.

'Here,' he said. 'What's your business? You canna come visitin' here today – you'd best jist take that vehicle out o' here.'

Gently wound down his window. 'Is the officer in charge inside?' he asked.

'Ay, he is, but that's no matter – you canna come in at any rate.'

'Oh yes, I think so,' Gently said. 'What's the officer's rank and name?'

'It's Inspector Blayne, but I'm tellin' you—'

'Tell Inspector Blayne two people want to see him. A Mr Gently and a Miss Merryn. Tell him they have information for him.'

The constable, a man with a plump, freckled face, hesitated a moment, mouth open, eyes searching; then he turned to slam back up the steps and disappear into the house.

'Phew!' Brenda whistled. 'Not exactly an open-arms welcome. Are you sure we still want to help the natives?'

'The rain doesn't help their tempers,' Gently shrugged.

The constable returned. 'A'richt,' he said. 'The Inspector will gi'e ye five minutes. But jist the same ye can take that vehicle and park it properly, like other folk.'

'Oh, pull some rank,' Brenda said.

'I don't have any rank,' Gently grinned. 'Get out here by the porch. It'll save a belt through the rain.'

He parked the Sceptre by the police cars then they went on in. Beyond the massive front door, which was studded with bolt-heads, they stepped into a high, spacious hall. On their right a pine staircase, polished to a brilliance, rose to a gallery at first-floor level; and beneath the gallery, occupying most of that wall, was a mullioned window of stained glass. The floor was tiled black and white and covered in the centre with wool matting; and about the perimeter stood antique carved chairs, a carved chest and a huge carved cupboard. Swords, daggers, pistols and a pair of round shields hung in brackets on the walls, along with one or two vast, gloomy oil-paintings by Landseer or his imitators. Because of the weather only a dull light was issuing through the stained glass, so that when the constable slammed shut the outer door the hall was reduced to tinted twilight.

'You're to wait here,' he told them surlily, and went out through a varnished door by the foot of the stairs.

They peered about them.

'Gosh,' Brenda murmured. 'This is pretty lairdy, George. Just see those antlers hanging on the gallery – and that mossy bull leering out of the picture. Do they really have bulls like that somewhere, or is it a convention, like Chinese dragons?'

'Probably a convention,' Gently said. 'Any real ones would be at stud in South America.'

'Poor dears,' Brenda said. 'They'd so miss their

peat-bogs, and those lovely little rocks for standing their front feet on. How he's rolling his eyes, that big one. I wonder if he cut loose and chased the artist.'

Gently wandered over to a bracket of weapons. They were kept beautifully clean and oiled, he noticed. They were in no way fastened to the bracket and you could pluck out a sword or dagger at a second's notice. He lifted his hand to make the experiment, but then dropped it again with a grunt.

'Naughty,' Brenda said. 'I saw you do that.'

'Perhaps I'd better not put my dabs on them,' Gently grinned. 'But they're a lovely collection of murder weapons. I wouldn't want them around at Elphinstone Road.'

'Would the pistols work?'

'My guess is yes. At least, they're fitted out with flints.'

'Gawd. They'd make a fair old hole in you.'

'They'd do the trick. At short range.'

He passed on to another bracket, Brenda keeping close beside him. The hall had a quality of echoing silence that made one tread cautiously and speak low. In the darkest corner, a small recess in the same wall as the window, a helmet with chain cheek-guards stared emptily at them over a faintly gleaming cuirass.

'Compulsory Sunday lairds'-wear,' Brenda whispered.

'Shh,' Gently said. 'Someone's coming.'

Brenda listened. 'It's someone upstairs.'

'Yes, but they may have to cross over the gallery.'

Brenda's hand stole to his arm and they both stood

quite still. Soft, regular, slouched footsteps were approaching the gallery from the left. There was little light at that level and details of the gallery were indistinct; against what might have been a panelled wall one saw only the silhouette of the balustrade and of gigantic antlers. The steps sounded nearer. A flickering glow began to shine on the gallery. Then a woman appeared, carrying a candle, and apparently muffled in a big dressing-gown.

'God save us,' Brenda breathed. 'If she begins washing her hands, it's Lady Macbeth.'

'Quiet!' Gently hissed.

But the woman had heard them and, with a violent start, turned to look down.

For a second she paused, her hand on the rail, the candle lighting her smooth, pale face; then she continued to the end of the gallery and took some steps down the stairs.

'Who – who are you?'

Her voice was low, with the precise accent of an educated Scot.

'Just two visitors,' Gently explained apologetically. 'We're waiting to talk to Inspector Blayne.'

'Inspector Blayne. Then you know something—'

'We think we may know something about the accident.'

Her lips trembled. 'But it wasn't an accident.'

'Then whatever it was.'

'They murdered Donnie!'

Her mouth crumpled and tears began to overflow from her swollen eyes. She was not a beautiful woman.

Her nose was too thin and made too sharp an angle with a broad forehead. But she had a finely-drawn jaw and a small, vulnerable mouth, and these, along with a full cheek and a flawless skin, gave her face distinction and interest. She had plentiful dark hair worn straight and long. She was rather under middle height. Her age was perhaps thirty.

'They didn't need to. They didn't. They didn't. Donnie wouldn't have done them harm. Things might just have come and gone. At the worst . . . at the worst . . .'

'We're very sorry to intrude,' Gently said quietly.

She stared at him wildly through her tears. 'Ay, you're sorry,' she said. 'What would that cost you? It's no grief to the lookers-on.'

'We'd like to help—'

'You can't help. It's all done, done, done.'

'We may be able to help Inspector Blayne.'

'Two English folk! Never!'

But then she shrank a little from the rail, her eyes narrowing at Gently.

'What is it you think you know?' she said. 'What can you know – about Donnie?'

Gently shrugged. 'Nothing,' he said. 'I never met Mr Dunglass.'

'Then who is it about?'

'Perhaps nobody.'

'You can't have any tales to tell about me!'

Gently shook his head and said nothing. The woman's eyes clung to his. The candle, which she was still grasping, trembled and spilled grease into the stick.

Then she burst into sudden sobbing and ran back up the stairs and along the gallery. They heard a door open and slam, the creak of a spring, and silence.

'Glory!' Brenda exclaimed. 'What do you know about that? They've got a pippin of a case here, George. It should make the Sundays. Do you think she did it?'

'What do you think?'

'She'd be top of my list. She was scared silly, you could see that. And half those tears were for your benefit.'

A thin cough sounded behind them, making them turn quickly. A door had opened near the front of the hall and in the doorway stood a man.

'Aweel,' he said in a dry voice. 'Alistair Blayne, at your service. If you're through interviewin' Mary Dunglass, perhaps we can get to your bit of business.'

He coughed again and came out of the doorway.

'The lady has been lately widowed,' he said. 'The doctor has given her a wee sedative, but it doesn't seem to be doin' its duty.'

CHAPTER FOUR

I'se uphaud (him) for . . . the bitterest Jacobite in the
haill shire.

                 Rob Roy, Sir Walter Scott

INSPECTOR BLAYNE LED them along a passage a little less
gloomy than the hall and into a well-proportioned
room furnished as a library and study. The walls had
been regularly shelved with oak and red pine, the latter
forming the frames of doors and cupboards and the
panelling that ranged at the lowest levels, and the shelves
exhibited a catholic bookscape that stretched from folios
in sheepskin, through various degrees of calf, boards,
cloths, to the jazzier outsides of the present day. Old
estate maps in Hogarth frames hung at intervals of the
shelving, and a small collection of printed maps was
grouped above the wide hearth; a huge desk, a table, a
print-stand, a globe, an orrery and half-a-dozen solid,
leather-seated chairs completed the inventory.

When they entered it was apparent that a search was
in progress. Cupboard doors hung ajar and files and

loose papers were strewn on the floor. At the desk, where an oil-lamp with a pearl-glass shade made some impression on the prevailing dim-out, a sharp-faced man with sleeked hair was flicking through the pages of a ledger.

'A'richt, Purdy,' Blayne said. 'You may as well be off back to Balma'. Just do those one or two jobs we were talkin' of – and give me a tinkle when you're back, man. You can draw off a couple of men with you.'

'Shall I take this buik, sir?' Purdy asked, pointing to a folio bound in blue cloth, which lay on the desk.

Blayne fingered his chin. 'No, I think not. No, you can leave the buik with me.'

Purdy left. Blayne, with his own hands, dragged two of the chairs up to front the desk, flicked the seats with his handkerchief and waved his visitors to them. He was a tall, lean, gangling man who threw a stoop into all his movements, and whose very large hands, with very long fingers, fluttered vaguely when he spoke. He had a long skull and a longer jaw and lank, colourless cheeks, and his hair, bushy but cut short, was a curious pepper-and-salt mixture. Though he was probably younger than Gently his face suggested he was far older; yet his odd, springy motions had an air incongruously youthful. He took the seat Purdy had vacated.

'Well,' he said, laying his palms together. 'First, an apology about the lighting. I hear the line is down at Glen Liffin, so we're gettin' no current this side of the river. There's been a deal of rain, you ken – sometimes it starts the rocks movin'.' He gave Gently a sly glance. 'Ay,' he said. 'Well, that's that. Now we come to your own business. What were those two names, again?'

46

Gently repeated them and Blayne wrote them down, his large fingers travelling slowly; then he added their London addresses and the address of the cottage. When he'd finished writing he remained staring at the paper.

'Ay,' he said. 'Miss Brenda Merryn – a bonnie name. And *Mr* Gently.'

'That's correct,' Gently said.

'Oh, correct right enough,' Blayne agreed hastily. 'A proper modesty becomes a man – there's no two opinions about that – and in a manner you were leaving Rome behind you when you set foot across the Wall. Ay, *Mr* Gently I have it down here. It'll be so on the record.'

Gently chuckled. 'All right,' he said. 'I was just stressing I was on holiday.'

'And you've a perfect right, man,' Blayne said. 'You won't want to be concerned in our up-the-glen affairs. But well, we're not all that remote here from the likes o' papers and the telly and what with one thing and t' other – I knew fine who you were.'

'Ah, fame,' Brenda said.

'It makes no difference,' Gently said. 'As you said, I've left Rome behind me. I'm just a private citizen in Strathtudlem.'

'No, no, not quite that either,' Blayne said, sawing his hands. 'You can't stop bein' who you are, man, by changin' banks at the Tweed. And here am I with a wee bit homicide, and you come knockin' at the door – you can't just be *Mr* Gently – a whiff of the Yard must step in with you.'

'Then it'll be a small whiff,' Gently said. 'I'm here merely with information.'

'Ay, and that's a rare enough item,' Blayne said. 'I'm obliged to you – obliged. But I'll put it this way: holiday or no – north of the Border or no – the likes of you will be for havin' the facts of any wee murder you run against. You'll be seein', thinkin', wonderin' where a private citizen won't – and coming up with your own notions – how far am I out?'

'You're not out at all,' Brenda said. 'That's a perfect picture of George on holiday.'

'So I'm thinkin',' Blayne said. 'I was listenin' to him talkin' to Mary Dunglass. And now he'll be half-way into the case, just by hearin' her rant for a couple of minutes – and if you ken she has guilty knowledge, man,' he said to Gently, 'there's information I'd be glad to have from you.'

Gently hunched a shoulder. 'I couldn't tell that. I don't have details of the affair. She implied there was more than one killer and that she understood the motive.'

'Ay, that's no' new,' Blayne said, sounding disappointed. 'That's just what the lady's inclined to believe. And if it's the fact of the matter – I don't ken – there'll be small credit for Alistair Blayne. But if the lady was involved, now—'

'She's involved,' Brenda said. 'Personal opinion – one bitch of another.'

Blayne nodded seriously. 'That's my notion too, lass. But de'il any evidence I have to prove it.' He rubbed his great palms together, making a sound like rustling paper. 'Man,' he said to Gently, 'it's a behind-doors sort of day – will you no' spend an hour discussin' the matter? I don't know yet what you have to tell me, but I'm guessin' it's not in the nature of a hot pursuit – it'll likely come to hand as I put the facts to you – and you'll fit it together better than me. What do you say?'

'He says yes,' Brenda said. 'Don't let him argue himself out of it.'

'It would be a favour,' Blayne said. 'And you can't go places this weather.'

Gently sighed and looked out at the rain, which he could see steaming over a wide lawn.

'All right,' he said. 'Just for an hour – or till the rain stops. But that's all.'

Blayne took out a long, silver cigarette-case, from which the pattern was almost worn, and reached tremendously across the desk to offer it to Brenda and Gently. Brenda accepted; Gently refused and began filling his pipe. Blayne fitted a cigarette to a lengthy holder and took a light from the top of the lamp. Then he puffed fastidiously for some moments, a finger cocked above the holder, his lantern-jaw moving in time and his hollow cheeks growing yet hollower.

'Aweel,' he said at last. 'These are the short, sharp facts of the business. Dunglass was up the braes last night and some lad stuck a knife in his back.'

He sucked another few puffs, his sunken eyes small in the smoke.

'And we don't know why he was up there,' he said. 'And the rain has washed out track and trace.'

'When did it happen?' Gently asked.

'Eleven, twelve o'clock time, says the doctor. He was

49

cold and stiff when McMorris found him, which would be seven this mornin', thereabouts. McMorris is the Forestry ranger, you ken – they're early risers in that profession – and he'd be out walkin' the fences with his bag of tools – the sheep are no friends to young trees.'

'And it was up at the Keekingstane?'

'Ay, just there. Dunglass was lyin' on his face by the Stane. You'd think he was starin' through the nick at somethin' and come down face-foremost when he was stickit.'

'Just one blow?'

'Ay. A guid one. Straight in under the left shoulder.'

'And you don't have the weapon?'

Blayne shook his long skull. 'And we're no' likely to have it, which is more. If the laddie pitched it into the trees it'll just stay snug till thinnin'-time – you could scarcely get a dog in there – and it'll be buried under the needles.'

'Have you an idea what the weapon was?'

Blayne nodded slowly. 'Ay. A guess. From the nature of the wound – it was guid and clean – I'd say the weapon could be a dirk.'

'A dirk!'

'Ay. That's a kind of dagger that goes in a Highland-man's harness. They were fell free with them in the old days, but they're no' quite in the fashion now.'

'A dirk – like those hanging in the hall?'

Blayne's features twisted in a ghoulish grin. 'So you noticed them did you? – ay, you would. But it's not one of those was stuck in Dunglass.'

'Would they fit the wound?'

'Not far short. But you hadn't occasion to luik at them closely. If you put a light to them you can see the dust – they haven't been out since they were cleaned last.'

'Still, it's a coincidence,' Gently mused.

Blayne nodded again. 'That's my way of thinking. And I'll have more to say on the subject o' dirks – but every dog in his own kennel.'

He took a number of sapient whiffs and tapped the holder over a wastebasket. Then he surprised Brenda, who was staring at him, by a repetition of his grin.

'And you've found no tracks, no marks,' Gently said.

'None. The rain's taken care of all that. It's just streamin' rocks and bogs knee-deep and wee bit burns runnin' wild. There wasn't even any bluid, savin' a spoonful under the body. But Ferguson – that's the doctor – is of the opinion he wouldn't have bled much from such a wound.'

'For example, broken twigs,' Gently said. 'The rain wouldn't conceal them.'

Blayne sucked in his cheeks. 'What would that tell us? Dunglass could have snapped them as well as another.'

'Then you know of nobody else being up there?'

'That's so.'

'Say – Mrs Dunglass?'

'She says she wasn't. I have a statement from the house-keeper to the same effect – the lady was never out of the house.'

'Have you examined her shoes?'

'Ay, I did. They tellt me the lady was fond of the

braes. But all her stout shoes were dry enough – you can't give her the lie from them.'

'So,' Gently said. 'Dunglass goes up the hill, and we don't know why. Do we know when?'

Blayne's head wagged. 'In a manner of speakin', though not very precisely. Dunglass was in this room all the evenin' – his lady was watching T.V. in the parlour – then at 10 p.m., it may be later, he says he must drive into Balmagussie. And with no more about it, he gets in his car – the gardener sees him fetch it out – and is last seen crossin' yon bridge and headin' down the road for Balma'.'

'But he never actually went there.'

'That's impossible. We found his car nearby Halfstarvit – and that's on this side of the river, a guidish way along the back road. No, either somethin' happened to change his mind, or his goin' to Balma' was just a blind – he was soon back over the river and makin' his way up the hill.'

'To meet someone.'

'What for else?'

'A woman?'

Blayne sucked air through his teeth. 'Its a wearisome trystin'-place, that – and close on the mirk hour, you ken. Still, it could be a female, nonetheless – one of your mountain hizzies would make light work of it – maybe Dunglass was cheatin' on his lady and some gudeman took the old way with him. Ay, it could be that.'

'But you don't think it likely,' Gently said.

'Not so I'd put my Sunday sark on it, without a deal more than's showin' yet.'

'Of course, you'll have checked out McMorris and the servants.'

Blayne's head moved.

'Wha' about relatives?'

'Dunglass's family are around Glasgow – the lady's at Cuitybraggan, which is almost as far.'

'Friends and associates?'

'None in Strathtudlem. Dunglass was a foreigner here, you ken – and his lady is no' that much better, coming from half the shire off. I ken they have an acquaintance in Balma' – Purdy is away to luik into it – and they'll know some rich folk hereabout – just in a passin' sort of way.'

Gently nodded and drew on his pipe. 'So that's a round-up of the hard facts.'

'Ay,' Blayne said, drawing out the word. 'That's what we have, short of speculation. There's more to come, but I wouldn't dilute an honest picture with chancy opinions. You have the facts now – less whatever contribution you may want to give me.'

Gently puffed. 'Carry on,' he said.

'You'll reserve your information?'

'For the moment.'

'I kent you would,' Blayne said. 'A man like yourself is not for rushin' things. Weel – aweel. What we come to now is a bonnie exhibit to be showin' an Englishman. Take a luik at this buik, *Mr* Gently – you'll not have seen its like before.'

He picked up the blue folio and handed it across the desk to Gently. It was a fat, weighty volume, evidently made up from a high-quality paper. The binding was heavy buckram; on the front cover appeared a gilt dagger, and divided by the dagger stood the legend:

Let Him Who Scorns The Tartan/Fear the Dirk

'A canny crest,' Blayne said smoothly, leaning back and watching Gently. 'It's an old sayin', you ken that. But an old sayin' is whiles current.'

Gently rested the book on his knees and met Blayne's look with a curious stare. 'I'd like to see a picture of this Dunglass,' he said. 'And perhaps you can fill me in on his background.'

'Ay, I can,' Blayne said, moving some papers on the desk. 'But will you not dip into the buik? It's a grand privilege to handle that.'

'So I'm beginning to guess,' Gently said. 'But every dog in his own kennel, I think you said.'

'Man,' Blayne said, his features twitching, 'it's a pleasure to talk to you – a real pleasure.'

He uncovered a photograph and passed it to Gently. It showed a dark-haired, dark-eyed man of about forty. Dunglass had been handsome in a full-faced way, with large, bold eyes and a determined chin. He had a short neck and strong shoulders, and a mouth that was faintly derisive; the picture gave an impression of power tempered by intelligence but probably by very little humour.

'How tall was he?' Gently asked.

'Not above middle height,' Blayne said. 'But a solid, porridgy sort of a lad – he wouldn't be behindhand in a scrap. There's an oar hangin' up in one of the rooms which says he stroked an eight at Cambridge – that's answerin' two questions in one. You ken now where he was schooled.'

'Where did his money come from?'

'Och, they're a big family in the merchanting line – Dunglass and Ritchie, you may have heard of them – no lack of siller in that clan.'

'Was he in the firm?'

'Not to my knowledge. It would be before he drew up this way. He bought the estate soon after he wedded and settled down to bein' a gentleman.'

'Hm,' Gently said. 'Well, that sounds unexceptional.'

'Very unexceptional,' Blayne said drily. 'If yon buik told no other story. Am I to understand you recognize the crest?'

Gently shrugged. 'I could give you a guess.'

'That buik man, is the minutes of the chieftain-meetin's of the Scottish Nationalist Action Group.'

'What exactly is that?'

Blayne closed his eyes. 'Just the wuddiest lot of them all,' he said. 'The most mischievous, doctrinaire set of Home Rulers that ever disturbed the Queen's Peace. Nothin' goes on, from liftin' the Stone of Scone to cuttin' the power line to Balmoral, but the S.N.A.G. is either doin' it or settin' on those who will. And Donnie Dunglass, that stirrin' laddie, was company-secretary to the whole clanjamfry – a principal, you ken – a prime mover – the tongue o' the trump to them all, most like.'

'Is the organization illicit?'

'Not precisely licit nor illicit. We ken well enough

what they're about, but we can't nicely put a finger on them. They've powerful friends, that's true, and a deal of sympathizers and fellow-travellers – especially this side of the Forth – there's aye tinder up the glens.'

Gently tapped the book. 'But you'll have names here.'

Blayne drew air through his teeth. 'Aliases,' he said. 'We're dealin' with folk as canny as the wild-cats in the timber. Maybe some notions down there are treasonable, but you'll scarcely ferret them out of the terminology – it's all projects-this and projects-that, with a set of daft-like names attached to them. I don't know but we may make out a case for proscription – but what guid would that do? We'd only luik the bigger fools.'

Gently nodded. 'Certainly a problem.'

'Ay. And we must just rub along with it. Unless the laddies begin to play rough and carry their dirks point-foremost.'

'Is that the suggestion?'

Blayne's head wagged. 'That's the notion of Mary Dunglass. An' if you'll kindly luik up the minutes of the last meeting, I'll expound what put it into her head.'

Gently opened the book, and Brenda shamelessly edged her chair closer to his. The last entry occurred midway through and formed only a brief paragraph:

A Chieftain Meeting was called at The Castle by The Lord Thistle on Tuesday 14 June. Present: Hillman, Knockman, Burnsman, Townsman, Linnman, Pressman, Lochman, Shipman, Forestman, Strathman. Subject discussed: Gorseprick

Project. Voting: 9 in favour. Abstention: Strath-man. Project adopted.

'A pithy sort of style,' Blayne commented. 'I could wish some of my officers would get in the way of it – but that'll be education for you – it's no' all rowin' down at Cambridge.'

'Was Strathman Dunglass?' Brenda asked.

'Ay, just so,' Blayne said. 'And by the gracious bounty of Mary Dunglass we ken what was the project he wouldn't vote on. It stands against her word, mind – though I don't ken why she should lie – but the Gorseprick Project is a treasonable motion to train the ghillies and suchlike in guerrilla fightin'.'

'Guerrilla fighting!' Gently said.

'It gave me a shog too, man,' Blayne said. 'You wouldn't believe men in their sober senses would sit down discussin' and votin' for sich things. But that's what Dunglass tellt his lady – the only time he's tellt her anything – and that because – to give him his due – he wouldn't have horns nor hide of it. He kent fine it would bring us down on them where we had given them rope before – and when they wouldn't listen to cool reason, he upped and banned them – and resigned. So now you'll be understandin' the view his wife takes of the matter. They fetchit him out on some pretence then gave him the traitor's end of the dirk.'

Gently stared for a moment. 'Can we really credit that?' he asked.

'It's a guid question,' Blayne replied. 'I don't ken if we can or no'. On the one hand it explains Dunglass's actions, which nothin' else would seem to do – on the other, I cannot quite stomach the S.N.A.G. bein' plunged so deep in sedition. They're political, man – no' terrorists – no whisper o' violence before this. I'm fair flummoxed. I'm sore needin' the sight of a handle to lay my grip on.'

Brenda looked at Gently.

'Perhaps we have the handle,' Gently said.

'Then open the kennel, man,' Blayne said. 'A dog of any colour would glad my eyes.'

Gently told him of their brushes with the owner of the dark blue Cortina; Brenda described the man and identified him as the one they had seen at the Keekingstane. Blayne listened, his cadaverous face solemn and shadowed in the yellow lamplight, his fingers scrawling down notes on the sheet that bore their names.

'Aweel,' he said when they had finished. 'A useful canine this may be. You wouldna be puttin' a collar on him in the shape of the registration number of the car?'

'Sorry,' Gently said. 'We'd no occasion to take the number. It was a post-Motor-Show '64 model. That's the best I can do for you.'

'Och, we'll find it,' Blayne said. 'There'll no' be that many in the district – and no' but one with sich an owner. I'll give Purdy instructions when he rings.'

'You don't know who Redbeard is?' Brenda asked.

Blayne shook his head. 'But I'm wishful to meet him.'

'George thought he was a farmer.'

'That may be. Though he wasn't up yonder to bargain for kye.' He rose stiffly and put out his great

58

hand. 'Man,' he said to Gently, 'this has done me guid. Just talkin' the thing over with a man like yourself has helped me give it a glim o' perspective. Are you stayin' long in Strathtudlem?'

'For the fortnight,' Gently said.

'Then maybe we'll be meetin' again, whether or no' your mannie is mixed up wi' the case. There,' he said, as a chandelier above them splashed sudden light through the room, 'you bring illumination where you come, man – they've mended the line at Glen Liffen.'

Gently looked out at the still-dashing rain. 'I wish I could do the same for the weather,' he said.

'Och, I'm the man with that in my pocket,' Blayne said. 'Do you no' ken it'll be steamin' sun by noon?'

CHAPTER FIVE

– Judge how looked the Saxons then,
When they saw the rugged mountain
Start to life with armed men.
                    'The Battle of Killiecrankie'

GENTLY DROVE THE Sceptre no farther than the
bridge, below which the augmented river was
booming impressively, before halting for the ostensible
purpose of giving himself a fresh light. But while the
match was flickering over the bowl of his pipe he was
staring hard towards the Lodge which, across two
hundred yards of rainy strath, one could see glimmering
palely among its trees. Then he grunted and stabbed the
match into an ashtray.

'What do you think of Blayne?' he growled at Brenda.

'I like him,' Brenda said in a small voice. 'Even
though he's walked out of some Rowlandson cartoon.
But I don't trust him, of course.'

Gently grinned at her round his pipe. 'Why?'

'He was much too flattering. I think his object was
simply to get you off the scene.'

'Yes.' Gently nodded. 'Also I think he was holding back.'

'About Mrs Dunglass?'

'About Mrs Dunglass – and about where his sympathies lie in the matter.'

He tilted open a quarter-light, admitting the rumble and crashing of the river. Before them the wrack was thinning slightly to show the trees on the eastern braes. Rain drummed on roof and bonnet, rills gushed over the road to join the river, but the light was steadily improving. In this Blayne was likely to prove a true prophet.

Gently said: 'It was something he let slip about there being small credit in it for him – if Mrs Dunglass's theory was correct, and Dunglass was killed in some Nationalist quarrel. Of course, he might have meant the police would be unpopular if they hung a murder charge on the Nationalists. But he could have meant he didn't expect his investigations to succeed.'

'Because,' Brenda said, 'he has Nationalist sympathies?'

'It's not impossible,' Gently shrugged.

'An intriguing thought,' Brenda said. 'Now this sort of thing we just do not have in England. Perhaps he's one of the Hillman–Lochman clique himself.'

Gently chuckled. 'That's going too far. I reckon Blayne to be a loyal and efficient policeman, but not over-anxious to make trouble for the Nationalists. I think he's worried in case there's something in it and he can't avoid taking action. It's deflecting his attention from Mrs Dunglass – which is perhaps what it is intended to do.'

'Aha,' Brenda said. 'A red herring.'

'It was Mrs Dunglass who suggested Nationalists.'

'Yes – and who told the Inspector her husband had a row with them – and spun him a yarn about them training guerrillas. That's a load of old codswallop if you like.'

'But I'm not sure he doesn't believe it,' Gently said.

'Well I don't believe it,' Brenda said. 'I believe she's a scheming, conniving woman. I'll bet she's got the house-keeper squared, and the gardener too, if his evidence matters. And remember what her shoes tellt the Inspector – she'll know her way about the braes.'

'It may not be quite so simple,' Gently mused.

'Oh, she knows something,' Brenda said. 'For Heaven's sake listen to my intuition, George – she's as guilty as hell. Don't defend her.'

'I won't defend her. She's too pretty.'

'Oh,' Brenda said. 'And oh. And oh. Listen to this – she knew enough to use a dirk, to make it seem like the Mafia did it. What about that?'

'It only *may* have been a dirk.'

'She's got you,' Brenda said. 'Her bonny blue een. Wait till you read all about it in the papers my poor, sappy, simpering copper.'

'No, but seriously,' Gently grinned.

'Seriously she could have lured her husband up to the Stane. Seriously she could have followed behind in the dark and seriously bunged a dirk in his back.'

'What about Redbeard?'

'Another red herring. He's probably a stray train-robber, the way I supposed. He was going innocently about his unlawful occasions – I daresay checking on the Highland Mail.'

Gently shook his head, chuckling. 'We're away ahead of the facts,' he said. 'Let's start again at the beginning and take it along, step by step. First, we'd better believe Mrs Dunglass's story, because that's all we have to go on. She says her husband told her he had a telephone call and that he would have to go into Balmagussie.'

'So she'd ask him why,' Brenda said.

'All right,' Gently said. 'She'd ask him why. And he'd say something about business or the Party – she was perhaps used to him going off at odd hours. Anyway, he goes over the road to the garage, where the gardener also has his cottage, and the gardener sees him fetch out the car and drive away towards the village.'

'Over this bridge,' Brenda said.

Gently shook his head. 'No. The cottage lies behind the house and the trees from this bridge, so it must have been someone in the house who saw the car go over the bridge.'

Brenda glanced towards the Lodge. 'I see,' she said. 'Clever. That's why you stopped here.'

'It could be a very important point,' Gently said. 'I wanted to get it clear in my mind. Now even from the house, as you can see, it's difficult to get a view of the bridge. You'd need to be standing at that one special window and looking slantwise in this direction. So if Mrs Dunglass saw the car cross the bridge she was necessarily watching to see if it did, from which it follows Dunglass knew he'd be watched and took care he'd be seen heading for town. So now the situation is

Dunglass was bluffing about the trip into Balmagussie, and Mrs Dunglass was suspicious, and Dunglass knew she was suspicious.'

'Oh upright judge,' Brenda said. 'You're still knocking nails into her coffin.'

'From the first,' Gently said, 'Dunglass's object was a rendezvous at the Stane. He received a message requiring his presence there and it was important his wife shouldn't know where he was going. So he plays his bluff, drives off through the village, recrosses the river lower down, then takes a path from there up the braes and so to the Stane. He wouldn't have used the regular path because it starts too near the house – and the odds are we must have seen him, with the timing being so tight.'

'Please,' Brenda said. 'Let me go on. Question: Why was it important his wife shouldn't know? Answer: He was on secret Party business. Comment: His wife knew about his Party business. Question: What remains then? Answer: A woman period a woman – and if you come up with anything different, George, I'll scream and burst into tears.'

'I daren't risk it,' Gently grinned. 'But it's still a curious place for an assignation.'

'Not for mountain hizzies.'

'Even for them. There must be other and better places lower down.'

'You took me up there,' Brenda said. 'And I'm just a feeble Kensington hizzie. This one will be a wild, haggis-fed Highland female who can skip up and down braes like a goat.'

Gently sighed. 'All right,' he said. 'I concede a woman is the most likely answer. But we still don't know why she summoned him up there at such an unusual time, and at a moment's notice.'

'She must have had the urge,' Brenda said. 'It's probably the mountain air that does it.'

'Maybe. But why did he go? He apparently knew he was taking a risk.'

'Ah,' Brenda said. 'Young love.'

'There just could be a secondary reason – like blackmail. If he was having an affair he'd be open to blackmail – and a summons from a blackmailer would explain his caution.'

Brenda gave her corn-coloured hair a twist. 'George,' she said. 'Have it any way you like – as long as he went up there to meet a woman – and as long as Mary Macbeth went up and caught him at it. That's the plain crux of the matter. It's a slice of good old Frankie-and-Johnny. No guerrillaring ghillies or dirk-happy patriots – just straight, honest, wholesome revenge.'

Gently puffed. 'We'll agree on that. I think the Nationalist angle is a blind.'

'Stop right there,' Brenda said. 'Then I won't have to say I Told You So later.' She snuggled a little against him and slanted her face to his. 'Now forget it, George,' she said. 'Leave mighty Blayne to sort out the pieces. I want to get back to being on holiday.'

Gently smiled at her. 'Have you noticed anything?'

'No. I've been wasting my time talking.'

'It stopped raining two minutes ago.'

★ ★ ★

But when they got back to the cottage they found neither Geoffrey nor Bridget much inclined to stir. Geoffrey was painting; Bridget had her feet up and was knitting and avidly reading a novel. Geoffrey had his gear on the table by the window and was slopping about lushly with Prussian Blue. The braes had come into sight a moment before and he wanted to catch them before they vanished again. All the while Gently and Brenda were reporting their visit his brush was teasing, blotting, scrubbing, and at intervals he exchanged it for a palette-knife and scraped raw, smarting patches out of the pigment. But he was listening, and Bridget surmised and asked questions enough for two; and the subject continued until, to Geoffrey's chagrin, his inky braes turned suddenly green-gold, and there could be no more doubt that the morning's rain had finally retreated westward.

'Come on,' Brenda said. 'Let's get in the cars. It's still only half-past eleven.'

But Geoffrey looked wistfully at his unfinished sketch, and Bridget turned a page firmly.

'You two go out,' Geoffrey said. 'We were planning on lunch at the Bonnie Strathtudlem. We've had two days on the road, you know, and a day doing nothing would suit us best.'

So it was agreed, and Gently and Brenda set out again on their own, in a Sceptre with windows still misted and its Whitehall polish yet pebbled with rain.

They drove northward through the village between braes now flashing and brilliant with colour. A sky of soft blue fire extended above the sharp-etched tops.

Ahead, a group of more naked peaks were unfolding purplish cliffs and blued shadows, and to the left the Braes of Skilling, the tributary glen, lifted roundly and greenly above smoking thickets. Soon they came to Lochcrayhead, the village at the top of Glen Tudlem, from which Glen Cray and its burnished loch drove a wedge eastward through the hills; then they were up in the bare rocks and black crags of Glen Donach, where no man lived, and where the crooked road was blasted and riven from sheer cliffside.

'Where do we eat?' Brenda asked, the map unfolded over her knees.

'There'll be a hotel somewhere,' Gently grunted. 'Towards Loch Torlinn. We'll take that road.'

'There's the Leny Hotel under Ben Leny and the Vrachan Hotel under Ben Vrachan.'

'We'll see where we finish up. You can't go very far wrong in these parts.'

Brenda spread the map wider, and still it was blotchy brown panelled with blue. Occasional touches of grey, now growing more frequent, indicated peaks rising above four thousand feet. The roads were contorted and illogical and ruthlessly dictated by the massifs, and the place-names, except those by the roads, were uncouth and unpronounceable. If you strayed from the road you stepped into country as foreign as the moon. These few thin veins of red on the map were the only lifelines of civilization.

'It's a far country, and it keeps getting farther,' Brenda mused. 'Really, it's a shock to us poor southrons who live in and out of each other's pockets. We're used to thinking of our country as urban, with every square yard recorded and occupied – everything cosy. Then we drive up here and suddenly run slap into Outer Mongolia. It's almost frightening. It's like turning round to find your house has only three walls.'

'Doctor Johnson was much of your opinion,' Gently said.

'I'm not surprised,' Brenda said. 'They looked things square in the face in those days. It's all very well being sloppy and romantic, but a lot of mountains are a lot of mountains. You can't farm them, you can't make roads on them and they're full of violence and a sort of threat.'

'They're just rocks,' Gently said. 'Weathering away in their own weather.'

'So why do we come gawking at them?' Brenda said.

Gently grinned. 'Well . . . they're there.'

They came down out of Glen Donach and bowled along a strath road into Kinleary, a prim, stone-built town with a torrent funnelling under a graceful bridge. Its main street was very broad and the houses were capacious and large-windowed; it had an air of detachment, as though waiting for something to happen. Beyond, the road climbed again for its fifteen-mile stride beside Loch Torlinn, and looking back one saw Kinleary riding its image in a bay of the loch. The lines of the mountains and the loch converged on it in a Turner-like construction, and the tidy, austere little town now showed an aspect of extravagant beauty.

They met little traffic. The road stayed high, with emptiness always at its elbow. At long intervals they would pass a cottage, where a steep path would sag down to the loch-shore. Across the loch, at the width of a mile, the braes were thinly planted with deciduous trees, giving the effect of a vast park rolling endlessly along with them. The peaks behind the braes were dark, their faces to the loch being in shadow; and between them one caught glimpses of peaks yet more wild and inaccessible.

At last they could see the loch ending squarely and rather tamely at Torlinnhead, and a sudden sharp turn and descent brought them into the village. There was one hotel, the Honest Highlandman, whose sign represented a clans-man carrying his head; Gently ran the Sceptre into the yard behind it and they went in to lunch.

At coffee, which they drank alone in a lounge that faced straight down the loch, Brenda unfolded the map again and began poring over routes. Because of the arbitrariness of mountain highways they had either to return the way they had come, or make an extensive circuit back to Lochcrayhead by way of Logie, Bieth and Ardnadoch.

'Of course, its all ravingly beautiful,' Brenda frowned. 'But I just don't like having it forced on me. I'm tired of going longways through the glens. What I want now is a bit of sideways.'

Gently looked at the map. Their line of red certainly offered no alternative. It stretched crookedly and compulsively to Logie, and only to Logie would it go. But reaching south-east from Torlinnhead was a rambling, hatched double line, crossing direct over the massif top of Glen Knockie. He put his finger on it.

'There's your bit of sideways.'

'Oh my gawd,' Brenda said, looking. 'That'll be another of those "guid paths" – and a really hairy one this time.'

Gently referred to the legend. Its grading stopped at 'Other Serviceable Roads' which came below 'Roads Requiring Special Care'; neither were indicated by hatched lines.

'Not much encouragement,' he grimaced. 'But it must be some sort of a road. Look, there's a farm or something along it. The hatched lines probably mean it's unfenced.'

'Why,' Brenda said, 'don't I keep my big mouth shut.'

'We could just take a peep at it,' Gently grinned.

'We could just jump in the loch,' Brenda said. 'Oh, George, I took you for a *restful* man.'

But the hotel-keeper confirmed the road was 'no' a' that a bad ane', and spoke lyrically of the views they could expect 'off the tap'; so the Sceptre, after idling along the road by the top of the loch, ignored the broad way to Logie and turned its bonnet to the mountains.

The road began deceitfully. It was at first a lane sheltered by high, English hedges, apparently leading only to a barn which stood blocking the way ahead. Then it turned, narrowed, lost its metalling, lost its hedges, lost its innocence; became at one stroke a brutal rock-track with a gradient that made Brenda catch her breath. Gently slammed into second and the Sceptre grovelled its way upwards. The ground fell away sharply on the right, to the left rose menacingly above them.

The Sceptre moaned and bumped and grumbled, heaved itself round an S-bend, lifted its bows to a suicidal hairpin, stalled, and refused to restart.

'And that's that,' Brenda said. 'You'll never get her out of this, my son. You can't go up and you daren't back down – you're stuck, period. And serve you right.'

'I'll have to drop her back,' Gently said. 'You can get out if you like.'

'Oh,' Brenda said, 'I'll die young too. This or the bomb, it doesn't matter.'

Gently took reverse and very delicately braked-and-powered the Sceptre down. Then he restarted on the lesser gradient, and this time the Sceptre gnawed round the hair-pin.

'Which is more than you deserve,' Brenda commented scathingly.

Gently chuckled and kept going.

The track improved. Obviously the trick had been to get through the steep going at the commencement. Now they rose by straight, moderate gradients which the Sceptre took easily in second. Hill-pasture, grazed by sheep, swelled up on the one hand and lapsed gently on the other, permitting, as they climbed, a series of viewpoints into a tremendous glen eastwards. The glen was filled with trees but at times one glimpsed a river serpenting through it, and twice they caught sight of a castle, or castellated house, suggesting a picture snatched from a child's book. Then the glen receded behind the expanding hillside and suddenly was gone like a dream.

They came to a fieldgate of steel tube and beyond it the track levelled between shallow banks. On the left, among stunted trees, was the farmhouse Gently had seen on the map. It was a respectable, two-storey, stone-and-slate building occupying a site in a fold of the tops, with nothing but its ragged oaks and thorns to suggest the location was out of the ordinary.

As they approved it they heard a rushing and barking and sheep came pouring out of a gateway. A flock of them spread across the track in a trotting river, sweeping round the Sceptre and forcing it to halt. Men, dogs appeared, running. A youngster dashed along the bank to open a gate. There was an uproar of baa-ing, barking, shouting, along with the rustling drum of small hooves.

'Foo!' Brenda murmured. 'Truly rural. I'm not sure I appreciate tweed on the hoof.'

'Hush,' Gently muttered. Perhaps we're not welcome ourselves. The gaffer over there seems to want a word with us.'

An erect, hard-faced man, dressed in a sagging jacket and muddy jodhpurs, stood apart from the others, waiting for the sheep to go by. When they had cleared the Sceptre he came striding over to it. Gently wound down his window. The man stared at him, at the car.

'Are ye freends o' the laird's, like?' he demanded, tapping his palm with a thick ash-stick.

'Just tourists,' Gently said. 'This is a public road to Glen Knockie, isn't it?'

'Ay, you may say it's public,' the man said, his eyes roving about the back of the car. 'But it's not a usual road for tourists – who would be puttin' you on to it, now?'

'We saw it on the map,' Gently said shortly.

72

'Ay, it's on the map, that's richt.'

'And we wanted to try something out of the way.'

'Somethin' out o' the way,' the man repeated. He caught his palm a smack. 'Ye ken where ye're off to?' he asked.

'To Glen Knockie.'

'Very true. But d'ye ken through what sort o' country?'

Gently shook his head.

'I'll jist tell you then – in case your map didna give ye the information – ye're headin' into a deer-forest, man – so go canny – that's a'.'

He stared again at Gently, very hard, then turned to follow after the sheep.

'Hold on a minute!' Gently called. 'What's so special about going into a deer forest?'

The man came back. He bent down to the window. 'Either ye ken or ye dinna ken,' he said softly.

'I don't ken.'

'Then no harm's done. Jist hauld to the track like a douce mannie – it's a guid road if you take it quietly – jist go your ways down Glen Knockie.'

He strode away, his stick swinging, and began shouting unintelligibly to the others. Gently shrugged and looked at Brenda, who made a face and shrugged back.

'There's no doubt about it – we *dinna* ken,' she said. 'Do we go on?'

'We go on.'

'That's my man,' she said. 'Damn the torpedoes.'

The track still continued to climb, though at a much

easier rate; but the extreme roughness of the surface prevented Gently from raising the pace. They were well on the tops now and the pasture had given way to heathy moorland, a dark, sad, desolate plain enclosed by rounded shoulders and fretted rockrims. It was high. There was a shelterless bleakness that carried a sure stamp of altitude, though no contrasting depth was at hand for reference. Vegetation was scant, loose rocks and boulders were plentiful; bare rashes of rock and peaty soil showed picked and scoured by violent weather. A few curlews, tame as sparrows, were all that stirred on the tops. They rose limping-winged to sail a few yards, their liquid yelping sharp and spirit-like.

'I keep watching for the deer,' Brenda said. 'But I'm darned if I've seen a single antler. And I keep watching for a forest, but the last trees we saw were at the farm.'

'Perhaps a deer-forest isn't what we think it is,' Gently said.

'I think it's a forest with deer in it,' Brenda said. 'That's the impression one gets in Hampshire.'

'Well, perhaps the car scares them away.'

'Perhaps,' Brenda said. 'And perhaps.'

They bumbled on, and even the curlews seemed to be losing heart and falling behind them. For huge distances in every direction the black, boulder-strewn plateau stretched away. To the west a declivity was appearing, slanting in from between two shoulders, on a line suggesting that eventually it would converge with the track. Brenda compared it to the map.

'I think we're getting there,' she frowned. 'That ravine would probably be the beginning of Glen

Knockie. In about a mile we'll be going down – there's a delightful double-hairpin – then we cross a bridge, and it's level strath: about twelve miles to the main road.'

'It's always twelve miles,' Gently grumbled. 'That's standard measure in the Highlands.'

The declivity broadened and deepened, and revealed a stream gushing down its bottom. Soon the track joined it to begin a sharpish descent along its flank. The ground fell away on the right and a vista of glen began to grow, with a carpet of tiny trees, oaks and ashes, and level panels of pasture. They came to the hairpins. It was a rugged step of a corner with violent wrong-way cambers. Gently dropped to first, clawed in, out, in and out again. Then his nearside front wheel touched the heathy verge and dipped suddenly. Before he could react, the rear wheel followed – and the Sceptre listed to a halt.

'Now you've done it,' Brenda said disgustedly. 'You'll never get out of this one, George.'

Gently switched off and climbed out ruefully to inspect. The wheels had run into a mud-filled gully which the heath had effectually hidden from view; they were in to the axles, and the side of the car was canted hard against the bushy heath.

'We're stuck – aren't we?'

Gently nodded reluctantly. 'I'm afraid it'll take a tow to shift her.'

'And where,' Brenda said, 'do we get a tow from – in the middle of nowhere, West Perthshire?'

'Perhaps there's a farm—' Gently was beginning, when an unexpected sound cut him short. From the glen below a series of ragged, quick-fire shots had echoed up.

He stared at Brenda. 'Bring the glasses,' he said, and moved quickly across the track. Beneath, at a distance of perhaps half a mile, he spotted a house standing in a wide clearing. In front of the house were a group of men. A man was running across the clearing. Then the man fell, and shots sounded again – six, accompanied by a faint whiff of smoke.

He grabbed the glasses from Brenda and focused them on the house. There were eight, ten men, dressed in a grey battledress and armed with rifles. As he watched another man began to run, apparently following some obstacle course, to throw himself down, his rifle smoking, the sound of shots dragging behind it.

'My God,' Brenda gulped. 'So there aren't any guerrillas up the glens!'

'Here – look,' Gently said. 'It's just possible they're military or police.'

Brenda took the glasses and looked. 'Military or police my foot,' she said. 'This is Popski's Private Army doing their Operation Gorseprick. And another thing – this is Glen Knockie – and one of those aliases was Knockman. George, we've stumbled into a wasp's nest. You'd better get us mobile quick.'

A sharp, metallic rap sounded behind them, making them jerk round suddenly. Beside the Sceptre stood a man in grey battledress. He had a rifle. He was pointing it.

CHAPTER SIX

Will ye no wait for Tammie Laurie,
  Laird o' a' our scaur an' fell?
    Later Border Minstrelsy, ed. McWheeble

A N' HAVE YE a guid view for your keekin' – or will
you gang down a bit closer?'

He was a young man, not more than eighteen, a head
shorter than Gently, but stockily built. He wore a slouch
bonnet over his carroty hair and a cartridge belt about
his middle; he had a broad, freckled, squash-nosed face
with a wide mouth and sharp hazel eyes. On the sleeve
of his tunic was sewn a stripe and above it appeared the
letter K. On his bonnet, securing the band, was pinned
a badge: it was the silver dirk of the S.N.A.G.

He stood with a sort of careless alertness, his right
hand curled about the rifle's trigger-guard. Where he'd
come from was a mystery, because only the open
braeside stretched behind him.

'Suppose you stop pointing that gun at us,' Gently
said. 'We don't want an accident to happen, do we?'

'You needna fear that,' the youngster said scornfully. 'When this gun gangs aff it isna an accident. But get on wi' your spying' – it's whit ye're here for – an' there's plenty to spy at down at the house. Put thae bonnie glasses to your een an' see what's stirrin' up Glen Knockie.'

'You're mistaken,' Gently said. 'We didn't come here to spy. We're simply tourists who've had a mishap and need some help with our car.'

'Simply tourists, the man says!'

'Have you reason to think otherwise? Naturally, when we heard the shots down there we looked to see what was going on.'

The youngster cocked his head to one side. 'An' I'll be for believin' that, won't I?' he said. 'I'm jist a puir, innocent, up-the-glen laddie who'll take in whitever an English cratur' tells me.'

'It happens to be the truth,' Gently said.

'Oh ay. Ye canna move on this road for tourists. They're aye slippin' their cars in that hole and pullin' out glasses to watch the house. But dinna waste yer lees on me, man – we kent fine ye were comin'. The laird is fresh back frae London wi' a note o' yer capers in his pooch. So what have ye to say to me now?'

Gently shook his head. 'You've beat me,' he said. 'I'll just repeat that I want a tow – and that you're handling that gun in a dangerous manner.'

'Ay – he admits it!' the lad said triumphantly. 'I catchit him in the act – an' he admits it. So he'll jist about turn, himsel' an' the leddy, an' shankit down to the house.'

'Have you any vehicles down there?' Gently asked.

'Nane o' yer business whit we have.'

'Well – a telephone?'

'No' that neither. Most like you'll be leavin' in a Black Maria.'

'A charming youth,' Brenda said. 'This is Scotch hospitality at its best and brightest. Do you think he'd shoot us?'

Gently shrugged. 'Perhaps by accident. But we need a tow, and that house is nearest.'

'All the same,' Brenda said, 'I don't fancy walking down there with Robbie Roy's gun stuck in my back. Perhaps his Highland courtesy will permit him to shoulder it – or whatever is the polite thing with a rifle.'

'I'll no' pu' up ma gun,' the lad said, flushing. 'Ye'll be for jumpin' me if I do.'

'Oh, we'll walk ahead of you,' Brenda said. 'Then you'll have plenty of time to murder us.'

'I'll no' put it up!'

'Then I'll no' walk. And you did so want us to act like prisoners.'

'Better do as the lady says,' Gently grinned. 'It's usually quickest in the end.'

The lad chewed his lip and stared at them, but Brenda clearly intended no compromise. So at last he growled sulkily: 'Och, weel – you canna rin very far. If you gi'e me your word – ye're to walk weel aheid – I'll pu' on the catch an' shoulder the gun.'

'So I should think,' Brenda said. 'Hospitality isn't all you're short of up the glen.'

She fetched her bag from the car, Gently locked up,

and they set off down. The lad marched after them rather shamefacedly, but with the rifle slung on his shoulder. The track bore left round rocky shoulders, bringing the house below more directly in view, and as they drew closer the firing ceased and the men stood watching the three of them come down.

'It's nice being important like this,' Brenda murmured. 'But I can't help feeling we've strayed out of our century – or into someone else's newsreel. Do you think they waylay all their visitors?'

'You heard what our friend said,' Gently said. 'He apparently takes us for someone else.'

'Perhaps you look like Bonnie Prince Charlie,' Brenda said. 'Myself, I'm the spitting image of Flora MacD.'

They passed through a field-gate, then over a bridge, then right through double gates and a stand of tall oak-trees. The house, with several outbuildings and a paved yard, stood immediately beyond. It was an old building, roughly constructed from unshaped stone, but fairly large and with some pretension in its massive porch and big sash windows. The men had come round from their exercise ground and now stood in a group in the yard, facing them. They were mostly young men. They were dressed like the lad, with the same slouch bonnets and Nationalist badges. Stationed apart was an older man with chevrons on his sleeve and a feather in his bonnet; into his presence Gently and Brenda were marshalled by their captor, who straight-away launched into fluent Gaelic.

The older man listened, put questions, his eyes flitting about the two 'prisoners'. He had hollow features in the

Blayne cast, but narrower, with a pocked and weathered skin.

'So,' he said, when the lad had finished, 'you've been watchin' our sports, Dugald tells me.'

'Ay, they had glasses too, faither,' Dugald asserted. 'But they left them in the car, the cunnin' English.'

'Watchin' with glasses,' the man said. 'And where ye thought there'd be nane to see you – that's no' an over-friendly thing to be at – an' you two strangers in the glen.'

'Who am I speaking to?' Gently asked.

'Ane in authority,' the man said roughly. 'Ye ken ye're in Knockie – that's enough – ye'll ken more when it befits ye.'

'Can I take it you're the laird?'

'Ye cannot.'

'I should like to speak to him,' Gently said.

'So ye shall, ma mannie,' the man said. 'For ye'll ne'er stir from here till the laird returns.'

'Because – you're intending to detain us?'

'Ay – for a pair o' slinkin' English craturs – the same, no doubt, the laird was warned of when he was down-away in London.'

'Ha, ha,' Brenda said. 'I love this quaint Scotch humour.'

The man stared at her furiously and made a fierce sound in his throat.

'Look,' Gently said. 'Let's get this cleared up. You seem to be expecting people here who are not popular. If we have acted like two of them it was purely by accident – your laird could not have been expecting us.'

'Gould he not then,' the man snapped. 'And who preceesely do you say you are?'

'I'm a policeman from Scotland Yard,' Gently said. 'And this is a friend, Miss Merryn.'

'A polisman, is it!'

There was no question that Gently's announcement had produced an effect. The 'ane in authority's' eyes opened wide and there was a shuffling and murmur among the ranks. Dugald's mouth fell open to show strong but crooked teeth, and Gently was aware of several furtive and uneasy looks.

'Let's see your warrant-card, Mr Polisman.'

Gently took it out and showed it.

'Guidness me – Chief Supereentendent.'

'That's my rank,' Gently said.

'Ay,' the man with the feather said, his tone hardening. 'A bonnie rank – a bonnie station. But what's to stop you – for a' we ken – from forging sich a card as yon?'

'Oh, Heavens above!' Brenda exclaimed. 'Tell them to ring up Whitehall, George.'

'Och, ye ken fine that's just what we canna do,' the man said, turning on her. 'The nearest telephone is at Brig o' Shotts. Na, na – we've had them before – a surveyor from the Forestry was the last ane – we'll no be put off with printed paper an' a bit stamp an' a signature.'

'Then what do you want,' Brenda said. 'A royal commission in Gaelic?'

'For a start, no cheek from a bit English lassie.'

'Oh, romantic Scotland,' Brenda said.

Gently put away his warrant-card. 'All right,' he said. 'You don't believe us. Let's try to get at it another way – what people do you suppose us to be?'

The 'ane in authority' looked at him scornfully. 'I'm thinkin' you need small tellin',' he said.

'Still – I'm asking you.'

'Spies, man, spies.'

'But spies for whom?'

'For the southron rustlers.'

Brenda began to laugh weakly. 'George, this is just too much!' she gurgled. 'We'd strayed into a Vietnam news-reel before, but now it's changed to a 'B' Western. In a minute Cary Grant will ride round the corner – or Randolph Scott with a full posse – and we're the baddies, George, the wicked rustlers. I'll lunch out for weeks on it, back in Kensington!'

'So it's a laughing matter, is it, ma lassie!' barked the 'ane in authority', his long face paling with anger. 'It's just for fun when your London gangsters come slaughterin' deer in Knockie Forest?'

'Deer!' Gently said.

'Ay. Deer! With Bren-guns an' automatic rifles – an' trucks to haul the carcases away – and bluidy heids for those would stop them.'

'And this' – Gently waved a hand at the men – 'this is a counter-measure to the rustling?'

'What else would it be, Mr so-called-Polisman – what else have you come here to get a sight of?'

'Just that and no more – with those badges?'

The 'ane in authority's' eyes popped at him. 'Spies!' he spat. 'An' worse than spies. Dugald, throw thae English craturs into the game-store.'

'Wait,' Gently said. 'Illegal imprisonment is a very serious offence.'

'Listen to him, will you,' the man ranted. 'Daurin' the McGuigans on their ain sod. Away with them, Dugald.'

'And if we won't go?'

'Then there's those here will make ye.'

'At the point of a gun?'

'Ay – if need be – if ye canna be managed by main force.'

'Then we know where we stand,' Gently said. 'And what the charge will be when you're arrested. We won't resist. There's no point. But what we do now we do under threat.'

'What are ye waitin' for?' stormed the 'ane in authority'. 'Take them to the clink an' shoot the bolt on them. They can cool their heels till the laird gets in – he'll ken what to do with the likes o' them.'

Dugald – willingly – and three others – more doubtfully – closed about Gently and Brenda. They were marched across the yard to the rear of the outbuildings and up to a small bolted and padlocked door. Dugald had the key. The door was pushed open to reveal an ill-lighted interior. Gently stepped in, Brenda followed. The door slammed shut, and they were left in darkness.

They heard the bolt shot and the padlock clicked home, and the receding tramp of the men; then, except for their breathing, there was silence in the grubby-smelling gloom of their prison.

'The Land of Adventure,' Brenda said in her smallest voice. 'Why go to Tibet or Patagonia? Come to

Scotland for a Gothic weekend – no exchange or passport problems.'

'I'm sorry about this,' Gently apologized.

'Oh, it had to happen,' Brenda said. 'Somebody was bound to lock me up some day – I'm a *femme* who's so obviously *fatale*. And it was me who got his Highland goat.'

'No,' Gently said. 'It was my crack about badges.'

'Dear heart,' Brenda said. 'Let me have the credit. I made him go grey with my Western giggle. Shall we be in this niffy hole for long?'

'Maybe only till MacAdolf simmers down,' Gently said. 'He was rather too quick to discredit my credentials. I don't think his men are happy about it.'

'Oh George,' Brenda wailed, pressing against him. 'I don't really enjoy being locked-up, you know.'

'It isn't amusing, is it,' Gently said.

'Not amusing at all. Not the weeniest little.'

She snuffled in his shoulder for a while, and he stroked her soft, swingy hair. Now that his eyes were beginning to adjust he could see their place of confinement wasn't wholly unlit. At the farther end was a small window or grating, apparently protected with perforated zinc, and from this enough daylight soaked in to reveal whitewashed walls and a stone-flagged floor. The door had a drain down its centre and the walls were furnished with rows of hooks; there were also two rails suspended from the roof, each with its bunch of double-ended meat hooks. A game store: at all events, the Knockie deer were no myth.

'It's rather a puzzle,' Gently mused.

Brenda tossed her head and sniffed. 'Sorry,' she said. 'I'm not really a heroine, just an indoor girl with outdoor manners. What's the puzzle?'

'What's going on here. That yarn about rustling could well be genuine. It could be that poaching gangs send spies up here and that these people have had a tip-off. On the other hand the yarn would be a perfect cover for an Operation Gorseprick – and ghillies don't usually go around in battledress, sporting military insignia.'

'Or wearing silver dirks,' Brenda said. 'You got MacAdolf frothing with that one. No, George, it doesn't add up. Deer isn't all they have on their minds.'

'The yarn could still be genuine,' Gently said. 'It wouldn't be a less effective cover. In fact, it would be ideal to have an explanation that would stand up to official scrutiny.'

'But you know, I know,' Brenda said. 'And worst of all, MacAdolf knows we know – that what we saw wasn't entirely to do with deer-protection, and wouldn't stand up to official scrutiny. So what's he going to do about that?'

Gently chuckled. 'He's probably wondering.'

'Yes, and I'm wondering too – and the more I wonder the less I like it.'

'So,' Gently said. 'Perhaps it would be wise to help the man with a solution.'

'How do you mean?'

'We'd best get out of here – through that window, if we can unlock it.'

He went to the window, struck a match and examined the zinc and the wood framing. Then he took out a pocket knife and began prising up the zinc with the blade.

'But that's no use,' Brenda said. 'Look – bars.'

'Patience,' Gently said. 'One step at a time. I've an idea those bars are to keep people out – which is rather different from keeping them in.'

He worked away till he had about a third of the zinc loosened at the top of the frame, then he grasped it with both hands and ripped it down and off. Behind the zinc were two vertical bars which had been improvised from gas-piping. The flattened ends of the bars were concealed by the light frame which had carried the zinc. Gently tackled the frame. It was secured with panel pins and the pins were driven into solid deal, and although he could insert the knife-blade under the pieces he was unable to lever them clear.

'How about a meat hook?' Brenda suggested.

Gently grunted and reached one down. It wasn't an ideal tool for the job, but eventually it did what the knife-blade wouldn't. Then the ends of the bars were revealed. They had simply been drilled and screwed to the main frame. The screw-heads were rusted, but whoever had inserted the screws had touched them with grease for easy driving, and now they yielded with equal ease to the screw-driver stub on Gently's knife. The bars lifted out; the window was clear. Beyond it was a hazel-copse, then tall trees.

'Now we'll just reconnoitre . . .' Gently said, thrusting his head and shoulders through the window. 'Right . . . ladies first. There's a six foot drop: hold my hands, and I'll ease you down.'

He helped Brenda into the window, lowered her, then himself. They crept through the copse. All was silent. They reached the cover of the trees.

The trees extended from the rear of the house to the lower slopes of the braes, and stretched southward along the glen in a broad, dense belt. The going through them was far from smooth. At the strath level there was bog and underbrush; higher up, crag and outcrop, and rills which sometimes swelled to torrents. When they were clear of the house Gently called a halt. They had reached a ridge where the trees were thinning; below, to the left, they could see the roof of the house, to the right a section of the road down the glen.

'What now, O Highness?' Brenda inquired.

Gently shrugged. 'I'm darned if I know. Unless we just keep plodding through these trees till we get to the other end of the glen.'

Brenda shook her head. 'Twelve miles, remember? I'd settle for hoofing it down the road – but not through the trees. That's out. You'd have to carry me over the last ten.'

'Well, the road's out,' Gently said. 'They're sure to check that when they miss us. And we can't go the other way, up the track, because it's in full view of the house. What we seem to need is a vehicle.'

'The oracle speaks,' Brenda said. 'And the glen, of course, is littered with vehicles.'

Gently nodded to the house. 'They've got one there.'

Brenda rolled her eyes; but just then the sound of firing broke out again: the same irregular pattern of shots that had first attracted their attention. Gently caught Brenda's arm.

'Right,' he said. 'That settles it.'

'Settles what?'

'I'm going back down there to pinch that Land Rover I saw in the coach-house.'

'You're mad,' Brenda said. 'Oh, quite mad.'

'Not now they've started their shooting again. They'll all be round at the back of the house. I can simply walk in and drive away.'

'They'll have left a guard somewhere.'

'Why? They think we're still locked up in the game-store. At the most they'd put a guard on that, and he'd be out of sight of the front of the house. Look: here's the plan. You make for the road and keep out of sight till you hear me coming. I'll toot my horn so you know it's me, then you can show and hop in. All clear?'

'No, damn you. If you're going, so am I.'

'It's better my way.'

'The hell it is. What would I do if they caught you?'

Gently hesitated. 'Come on, then,' he said. 'Only remember – no heroics.'

'I'm no heroine,' Brenda said. 'I told you before. Just watching heroes is enough for me.'

Gently led the way, taking a line that would bring them round the side of the house. The firing continued reassuringly in evenly spaced bursts. They came to the edge of the trees. The house, the yard, lay deserted before them in the warm sunlight. Across the yard stood the open-doored coach-house. In its gloom they could see the grille of the Land Rover.

'If there's anybody in the house . . .' Brenda whispered.

'That's a risk we'll have to take.'

'How will you start it?'

'There are methods. If anyone's bothered to remove the key.'

They left the cover of the trees, moved swiftly across the yard. Nothing stirred. The blank windows of the house stayed blank. They reached the coach-house. It smelled of petrol and grease and old tyres, and there was space in it for a second vehicle and oil on the flags where one had stood. The Land Rover was newish and beautifully clean and had a 'K' in a circle painted on its bonnet. Shovels and pick-axes were strapped to its sides. The ignition key was in place.

'Watch the doors,' Gently muttered. 'They make a clang.'

'If you hear a clang it's my heart,' Brenda whispered back. 'Can we really get away with this?'

'Just get in. We'll know the answer when I start the engine.'

Brenda opened her door: but then she went stiff and pointed behind Gently with a trembling finger. Gently whipped round. One of the riflemen was standing big-eyed in the doorway. He was holding his rifle uncertainly across his body, as though to push them back into the coach-house with it, and his mouth was beginning to open in a shout for assistance. Gently walked straight up to him. The man pushed with the rifle. Gently grabbed it with his left and struck with his right. The side of his hand slashed into the man's neck and the man dropped like a sack, leaving Gently with the rifle.

'Oh glory!' Brenda gasped. 'You didn't argue with that one, did you?'

'Get in!' Gently snapped, setting down the rifle. 'He may have some pals close behind him.'

He jumped into the Land Rover, hooked out the choke and twisted the engine to raucous life. For two, three long moments he revved it before hitting the gear and letting go. The Land Rover bucked and roared out of the coach-house. Above the roar he could hear shouting. As he crashed through to second he glanced in the mirror and saw men running round the end of the coach-house.

'Duck!'

Brenda crouched forward in her seat just as the first hammer-blow struck them. Then came another, and another, striking low down at chassis level. The trees toiled towards them. Gently switched to third; the engine shuddered but clawed back to revs. Two more blows landed. There was a vicious hiss followed by a lurch and a violent rumbling.

'Goddamn those blasted marksmen!'

But now they were into the trees. The house, the running men juddered out of the mirror, and no more hammers struck the Land Rover.

'Oh, keep her going, keep her going!'

'No fear of that – if she holds together!'

Gently was having to wrestle the limping vehicle, but his foot still powered the skittering wheels. They yawed and bumbled through a clutch of curves, the burst tyre flogging viciously, then shot out on the level strath and began pulling steadily away. Gently eased off.

'Oh my God,' Brenda moaned. 'And me who's never been shot at in my life!'

'They weren't shooting at us,' Gently jerked. 'They were after the tyres – and they got one.'

'Can we keep going?'

'It may ruin the wheel.'

'Shame,' Brenda sobbed. 'Stop and change it.'

'What we don't know is whether they have transport.'

'You're such a comfort to a girl,' Brenda wailed.

The Land Rover rumbled and swooped and rolled but kept pegging down the narrow road. Trees crowded close to it on both sides and the surface was wavy and full of potholes. It crossed a stream by a primitive bridge then made a sharp turn to the right. As they took the turn they spotted a car ahead. The car was a Cortina. It was blue.

There might have been room to pass that car if the driver had wanted them to pass him, but obviously he didn't; he stopped squarely in front of them, got out, walked towards them.

CHAPTER SEVEN

Oh Mary was a wilfu' lass,
   An' didna what she should do
An' Angus was a lightsome lad
   Who did do what he would do.
     'For A' That's Come An' Gane', Lady Coupar

THE SHINE OF the Land Rover's windscreen probably concealed who was driving it, for the man who Brenda had dubbed Redbeard seemed suddenly to see them when he was a few yards away. He stopped abruptly. The expression of anger he was wearing faded into blankness. He stood irresolutely staring at Gently, a trace of colour in his wide-boned cheeks.

Gently climbed down from the Land Rover.

'You wanted to speak to me?' he said.

'Ay, I did.' The man nodded. 'And to anyone I find misusin' one of my vehicles.'

'You own this Land Rover?'

'Who else, man!'

'And the house back there?'

'Ay.'

'Then perhaps you'll favour me with your name.'

'I will. I'm James McGuigan of Knockie Lodge.'

He brought it out with a sort of growl that made it sound like a challenge. He was a massively framed man standing an inch or two over six feet. His face, immersed in the big beard, was handsome and in proportion, and his large, frank eyes an almost startling shade of blue. His finery of yesterday had been exchanged for a baggy jacket of rough tweed, an open-necked shirt and a pair of orange-stitched jeans.

'And you, man,' he said. 'Have I seen you and the lady before?'

'Seen us!' exclaimed Brenda, coming round the Land Rover. 'You jolly nearly ditched us at Baldock yesterday.'

'I don't quite recall that,' McGuigan said. 'But if it was so, I apologize. However, I do remember yourself comin' to keek at me when I was at coffee yesterday morning, and later leaving with this gentleman and two other people.' He paused, looking hard at them. 'That was so, was it not?'

'You bet it was so,' Brenda said. 'I wanted to see who it was who'd cut in on us like a maniac.'

'So may I trouble you for an introduction?'

'No trouble at all. I'm Brenda Merryn of Kensington, and this is Chief Superintendent Gently of Scotland Yard.'

'*You* are Chief Superintendent Gently!' McGuigan's large eyes jumped even larger. However little Gently's identity had impressed the others, it was going down big with the laird. He stood silent for some moments, his eyes fixed, his face expressionless. His big hands, which were covered with fine red hairs, opened and closed by his sides.

'So what are you doing up here?' he demanded suddenly. 'And who gave you permission to use the Rover?'

'We were hoping you'd ask us that,' Brenda said crushingly. 'And it's going to need some hard explaining from the Laird of Knockie.'

'And what would that mean?'

'It means this. We're a couple of harmless English tourists. But we've been ambushed, held at gun-point, insulted, threatened with violence, imprisoned and finally shot at – by the hospitable retinue of the said Laird. And this after he failed to get us himself by reckless driving on the A1.'

'What are you talking about, woman!' McGuigan exclaimed.

'It's the precise truth,' Gently said. 'We ditched our car up on the track, and directly a gun was pointed at us.'

'There are only my ghillies there, at target practice.'

'Yes, and we were the target,' Brenda said.

'What you say is impossible. They wouldn't have shot at you!'

'Take a look at the back of the Land Rover,' Gently said.

McGuigan flung away from them and inspected the vehicle. There could be no doubt of what he found there. He stalked back again, hands gripped behind him, and stood glowering towards the Cortina.

'Well?' Gently said.

'Did you say who you were?'

'We did.'

'Did you back it then – show them evidence?'

'I showed them my warrant-card, of course, but I was told it was probably forged.'

'Och, the damned lunatics!' McGuigan exclaimed. 'As though there's not enough trouble without this – by gar, I'll make some of them smart for it – go down on their knees – beg for your pardon! Did they say who they took you for?'

'They were kind enough,' Brenda said, 'to suppose we were spies for a gang of deer-poachers.'

'The daft gowks! You can't leave them two minutes – they're just children – you can delegate nothing. Ay, it's true,' he said, turning towards them. 'We're on the look-out for poaching bodies. I've just brought back some information that Knockie is due for a visit soon. So we keep our eyes open – our guns oiled. You cannot just rely on the polis. But to go misusin' tourists in this fashion – och, there's no excuse for it at all.'

'And that's your explanation,' Gently said. 'That you're merely preparing to repel deer-poachers?'

McGuigan looked aslant. 'It's no excuse,' he said. 'But that's the reason for how they handled you.'

'These men wore battledress.'

'It's a kind o' battle, man.'

'Military insignia.'

'Ay – they're children.'

'Badges.'

'What's the harm in badges?'

'Particular badges.'

McGuigan hesitated.

'Man,' he said at last. 'I can see your drift – and I'm a wee bit surprised at your information. If you were dropping hints like this to Hamish I can understand him acting rashly. But whatever you think you've seen up the glen – and this is an honest bit of guidance – just remember it'll stand up fine in any court of law in Scotland. Now you've been mistreated – that's sure, and you have a case there if you want to press it. But if satisfaction will answer your turn – come back with me, man, and you shall have it. What do you say?'

'A lot,' Brenda said. 'I want the guts of that man Hamish and his son Dugald.'

'You'll have it – they'll kneel and beg your pardon.'

'And I want the stripes off them.'

'Well . . . those too.'

'How about the badges?'

McGuigan wagged his head. 'Just any honest satisfaction you're wanting, Miss Merryn. But if that's all, let's settle this matter after the manner of Highland gentlefolk – each man his own mare, and the devil take the lawyers.' He looked anxiously at Gently. 'It'll save a deal of time and trouble.'

'It's a point, O Highness,' Brenda said. 'Besides, I'd like to see MacAdolf eating dirt.'

Gently shrugged. 'Very well,' he said. 'We'll settle *this* matter Highland fashion. Provided you salvage my car and fetch it down for me.'

'Och, it's as good as done, man,' McGuigan said.

He climbed into the Land Rover and shunted it

expertly on to the verge, then hurried to open the doors of the Cortina and stood by to close them when Gently and Brenda had got in. The Cortina launched off eagerly. McGuigan spared no subtleties on it. He drove stiff-armed, head back, beard jutting at the road ahead.

They had gone no more than a mile when they met Dugald running towards them. He had his rifle slung across his back and was obviously in pursuit of the Land Rover. McGuigan screeched to a halt and whisked down his window. He thundered Gaelic at the sweating Dugald. Dugald's eyes widened, his mouth gaped and he seemed to grow smaller in his damp battledress. After a final growl McGuigan reached through the window, snatched Dugald's stripe and ripped it off him. Then he held out his hand, and Dugald tremblingly unpinned his badge and gave it up. McGuigan dropped stripe and badge in Brenda's lap. Dugald set off running down the road again. McGuigan closed the window, revved ferociously, and sent the Cortina leaping away.

'Oh my!' Brenda murmured. 'That was really telling Dugald something.'

'I've sent him to fetch the Rover,' McGuigan growled. 'They'll need it to give your car a pluck.'

'Are you always so conciliatory with your men?'

McGuigan drove some way in a heavy silence. Then the corner of his mouth twitched, and he said:

'You're either the laird or no' the laird.'

They swooped through the curves near the house and braked smokingly for the gates. Here it was the misfortune of 'MacAdolf', or Hamish, to be in the way of his master's wrath. Hamish, having taken in the situation, seemed to be wanting to speak to McGuigan, but before he could more than open his mouth a peal of the Gaelic thunder silenced him. The same performance was gone through again. Chevrons, badge tumbled into Brenda's lap. At first Hamish looked sulky, then astounded, then stupefied by the storm that rocked him; and at last was reduced to staring at his feet, his neck as red as a turkey-cock's.

'Now, ye stupid, gangrel body, yell apologize,' McGuigan concluded in English. 'Down on your knees, ye glaikit fool, or ye're for Barlinnie, and I'll not hinder it.'

'But I'm tryin' to tell you—!' Hamish wailed.

'Tell me nothing – down on your knees! By gar, ye're in peril of a seven-year stretch, and ye'd still chop words with me. *On your knees!*'

Hamish, gurgling, went down on his knees, but the scene suffered an interruption. The figure of a woman had appeared in the yard, and now she came running down the drive towards them. Her eyes were for McGuigan. Her expression was one of happy yet anxious anticipation. She failed to notice Gently and Brenda in the flutter of her approach. Then she saw them. She turned pale and staggered. McGuigan sprang out of the car and darted to her. She shook her head and tried to push him away, but he swept her up in his arms.

'Jamie – no!'

'Mary – Mary!'

She struggled weakly in his huge embrace.

'Oh Jamie!'

'What is it?'

'I've betrayed you – Jamie!'

And she fainted away. It was Mary Dunglass.

McGuigan hoisted her up – she was only a feather to him – and hesitated a second; then he gave a jerk of his head to Gently and Brenda and went striding off towards the house. They got out of the Cortina and followed him. Hamish scrambled up anguishedly from his knees. He ran after his master and jigged along beside him, expostulating, twisting about to face the big man.

'Och, Knockie, if ye'd only listened! I was for tellin' ye – I kent she meant trouble.'

'No more of that, man.'

'Ay, but she tellt me – I kent fine about the vagayries ower at Tudlem.'

'Whist – hold your tongue.'

'But Knockie, I maun tell ye – the Englishman kens ye were up the braes!'

'Man,' McGuigan growled from his belly. 'If ye *winna* hold your tongue, by gar, I'll grip it an' stow it down your thrapple!'

In the yard stood a blue Sunbeam Alpine, presumably the property of Mary Dunglass. McGuigan marched past it and up the steps of the porch and crashed open twin doors with his boot. They followed him in. He carried his burden into one of the rooms and laid her tenderly on a sofa. She was conscious again now. She was staring at McGuigan, her eyes dark against her pale face.

'If I'm not mistaken,' McGuigan growled at Gently, 'you'll be wanting a word or two with us.'

Gently nodded. 'It could help if I understood certain matters.'

'Ay – but first the lady must get her breath back – and then we'll want some cracks of our own. You'll be good enough to bide in the sitting-room, man – I'll have Lettie fetch you in some refreshment. Lettie!'

A dour, mannish-faced woman appeared at the door to listen with downcast eyes to the laird's instructions. She made a tart little bob to Gently and Brenda and stood aside to usher them out.

'What about my car?' Gently asked.

'Give the keys to Hamish. He knows what to do.'

Gently handed them over; then they followed the dour woman to a room on the other side of the house.

'Offer me a cigarette,' Brenda said, when the door closed. 'George, this is upsetting. They really love one another.'

'I'm afraid they do,' Gently shrugged, offering his case. 'And not even a Scots jury is going to miss it.'

'McGuigan's a devil. He doesn't deserve her. And she's a daft bitch – she doesn't deserve him.'

'As you say, they're made for each other.'

'And now they're right up the creek.'

She accepted a light, began stalking the room and puffing out short jets of smoke. It was a dull room. It contained Victorian furniture that simply looked seedy and outmoded. High on the wall hung a large, grimy case from which peered a family of moulting wild cats; near the window stood a vast fretwork cabinet exhibiting dusty trays of geological specimens.

'My God, it needs a woman around,' Brenda nagged.

'Sit down,' Gently said. 'We may be here for a while.'

'But George, why didn't she marry the great oaf in the first place, instead of wasting her sweetness on Donnie Dunglass?'

'Perhaps she loved Dunglass.'

'Never in your life. She didn't love anyone before she loved Jamie. He's the guiding light of her frabjous existence, and if you don't know that you don't know anything.'

'It did strike me that way,' Gently admitted. 'But I was waiting to get an expert opinion.'

'Now you've got one.'

'Perhaps you can tell me something else. Do you like McGuigan – or don't you?'

'Hah,' Brenda said, straddling before him. 'The trained brain. I shall have to be careful. When you put a question to me like that I'm supposed to effervesce with mindless truth. I hate McGuigan. I hate his beard. I hate his size. I hate his vanity. I hate McGuigan with a fierce hate. And I like him very much. Will that do?'

'It seems adequate,' Gently grinned. 'Let me switch you to the lady.'

'Oh, she's just a fribbling, gipsyish thing,' Brenda said. 'I'd share my flat with her tomorrow, and pinch her stockings like nobody's business.'

'Neither, you'd say, is cut out for murder.'

'Jamie might frighten someone to death.'

'But not go after them with a dirk.'

Brenda shook her head decidedly. 'He'd sooner grapple them by the thrapple.'

'Of course, we could be wrong,' Gently mused. 'I've

dealt with some really likeable murderers. And it would be so convenient for Inspector Blayne to have such a clear-cut, uncomplicated solution. I daresay nobody will pull many strings on behalf of a pocket laird and his light-o'-love – not like they would for a Nationalist group, with its fingers in everyone's pie.'

'You're so beautifully cold-blooded about it,' Brenda said. 'Your noble professionalism slays me.'

'I'm just reviewing the situation as it stands,' Gently said. 'Blayne is human – and it may be his superiors are sympathizers with the S.N.A.G. If that were so, then his play with them this morning may have been a bluff for our benefit – a pretence that if they were really involved he would still do his duty without fear or favour. No policeman in his senses could overlook the other angle, and Blayne was appearing to do just that. Eventually, when he charges this pair, we will be expected to be satisfied that he gave equal attention to S.N.A.G.'

'But that would be a deliberate frame!' Brenda exclaimed.

'Not if McGuigan and Mrs Dunglass really killed her husband. It would just be a diplomatic deception to support the characters of Blayne and the S.N.A.G.'

'But Jamie and Mary *didn't* kill him.'

'Nor, perhaps, did the S.N.A.G.'

'Then who did?'

Gently lifted, dropped his hands. 'Some other party. Our friend X.'

'Oh, I hate being logical!' Brenda cried, beginning to stalk the room again. 'Nothing ever came of a syllogism except another syllogism. Facts, figures, slick arguments, they're just a mental screen against what is. I know what I know what I know – and Jamie and Mary didn't kill him.'

'This morning you were equally positive she had a hand in it,' Gently grinned.

'There you go again – demanding consistency! How did I know they were in love?'

'Doesn't consistency matter?'

'Of course it doesn't. It's simply the first fallacy of logic. What is is is when it it, and what is now is they are innocent.'

'I'll have to remember that,' Gently said. 'It must have some other applications.'

'Oh George, I'm unhappy about this business.'

Gently humped his shoulders and stared at the wild cats.

Lettie returned, as sullen as before, bearing tea on a tarnished tray. She laid it on the cabinet without a word but gave her eloquent bob before departing.

'How she loves us,' Brenda sighed. 'It was probably her who shopped us when we sneaked the Land Rover.'

'We're the enemy,' Gently said. 'She remembers Culloden.'

'Bannockburn too, I shouldn't wonder.'

But the tea was good, and there was a plate of scones still warm from the baking. They sat on low chairs with high, carved backs and sipped and ate and gazed at the room. It was a sad room, as well as a dull one. It smelled of disuse and straitened fortune. Nothing in it was new except a few books which lay stacked on a whatnot in the dimmest corner. Perhaps four generations had slipped away since that furniture had been new and modish, since the candles were lit and a Laird of Knockie had entertained guests with his fossils. Yes, it needed a woman around . . . especially, it needed a rich widow.

'I suppose . . . I suppose,' Brenda murmured.

Gently chewed a scone and said nothing.

They finished the scones and drained the pot. Soon after, McGuigan and Mary Dunglass came in.

McGuigan closed the door.

Mary Dunglass, with a deal more colour in her cheeks, slipped shyly to a high-back chair and sat droopingly to stare at the carpet. McGuigan stood. He found a post for himself before the rusty iron hearth, leaning back, elbows on the mantelshelf, his beard tilted at the world. He took a fierce look at Gently.

'Well, we've had our words, man,' he said tightly. 'We have this matter straight now. You can go ahead with your questions.'

'Just a moment,' Gently said. 'I don't have any right to ask questions. In Scotland I'm simply a private citizen – nobody is answerable to me.'

'You're acquainted with Blayne, are you not?'

'Only as the officer investigating a certain case.'

'Ay, and you talked it over with him, and gave him your mind – you ken the case as well as he does.'

'That may be so, but he's your man.'

'It's you I want to be asking the questions.'

'Please!' Mary Dunglass broke in. 'It's your help we're asking for, Superintendent. We're in sore trouble, Jamie and I – he's too proud to ask you, but I'm not!'

'Is that the truth?' Gently asked McGuigan.

McGuigan's beard stuck out even straighter. 'Ay,' he growled. 'She tells you true. We need your help, man – there's all that's to it.'

'But how can I help you?'

McGuigan scowled. 'You can hold us for innocent, for a start. And it's just that you're English an' have no standing that sets you where you can do that.'

'I'll have to inform Blayne of anything you tell me.'

'So you will – and so you should. But you need not think like him, none the more – you can pit your wit with Mary and me. You ken the case man, you're a grand expert, it should not be past you to get at the truth – an' the truth must be got at if we're to win out – we're dooms deep, man. Dooms deep.'

'Say yes,' Brenda said. 'Or I'll kick you, George.'

'Oh please, yes,' pleaded Mary Dunglass.

Gently wriggled his shoulders. 'Carry on then,' he said. 'As long as you appreciate my position – I can't hold out on Blayne.'

McGuigan lowered his beard and re-established his elbows on the mantelshelf. His large face, partly in shade, had an air of archetypal majesty. Though he was roughly dressed, his athletic build showed strikingly under his slack garments, and the shirt parting at his throat gave him a slightly coltish look.

'You ken Mary and I are cousins,' he said slowly. 'That's in the Scots way, you understand – she's a McGuigan from Cuitybraggan, which is over the hills – I spent a while there in my father's time. I kent Mary from a wee bairn. There's a year or two between us.'

106

'Ay, I grew up with Jamie,' Mary Dunglass said. 'He was at school with my brothers at Invergoyll. Then the war came, and Jamie was away and I didn't see him again for fifteen years.'

'I was in the Control Commission after the war,' McGuigan said. 'Then I was flying for Charter Airways. Then I was two years in Rhodesia. I didn't come back here till my father died.'

'To find your cousin married,' Gently said.

McGuigan nodded. 'The year before I got back. Dunglass was a cousin on her mother's side – they're a Glasgow family with big connections. And – I don't know how to put it – we just picked up again – Mary came visiting to Cuitybraggan. And Dunglass was cool, you'll kindly believe. He was not the mark as a husband.'

'Worse than that,' Mary Dunglass said bitterly. 'He was keeping some woman in Balmagussie. I won't blush for lovin' Jamie – I had a husband not worth two pins.'

'And so it went on,' McGuigan said, 'with a meeting now, a meeting then – till last night was once too often, I'm thinking, and some person tipped Dunglass the wink.'

Gently looked at Mary Dunglass. 'So you *were* up the braes last night,' he said.

She slanted her face from him. 'And if I was,' she said, 'it was no particular business of Inspector Blayne's. I didn't kill Donnie – I didn't ken he was there – by his own account he was off to Balma'. I had Mollie McGrath to swear I stayed indoors. Why should I tell the Inspector I went out?'

'You'll have to tell him now,' Gently said.

'It doesn't matter now. He's on to Jamie. And I ken

now what I didn't ken then, though I never did believe it in my heart.'

'That Mr McGuigan didn't kill your husband?'

She stared at Gently defiantly. 'Ay.'

'You thought it was possible.'

'I didn't believe it. But I didn't have it then from his own lips.'

She smiled at McGuigan, who remained stern.

Gently said: 'I want to know more about this assignation. Mr McGuigan only returned from London yesterday – how did you know he would be at the meeting place?'

'Och, it was prearranged,' McGuigan said. 'We fixed for one meeting at another. And coming north to Knockie you pass through Tudlem, so it was just certain I'd pause there when I was back from a trip.'

'You had no communication about it yesterday.'

'None.'

'Nor at all – since the meeting before?'

McGuigan shook his head. 'We had a manner of communicating, but nothing passed between us since we met last Saturday.'

'Would you care to explain what that manner was?'

McGuigan shrugged. 'It's no matter now. I used to ring Mattie Robertson – who keeps the Bonnie Strathtudlemand she'd pass the message to Molly McGrath. It's by ringing Mattie this afternoon I heard what had happened to Dunglass.'

'And you can trust these two ladies?'

'Ay, we can.'

'They're two of my own folk,' Mary Dunglass said.

'Molly came with me from Cuitybraggan, and Mattie's her cousin from Glencoram.'

'Then who do you think gave you away?'

'Neither of those two,' Mary Dunglass said.

'Then who?'

She shook her head. 'It was the person who rang him, I'm sure of that. He gave me an auld, auld look when he came to tell me he was away – he kent then – no' before – I should have taken warning from it.'

'And neither of you can guess who that person was?'

'We were always gey careful,' McGuigan said.

'Somebody who might want Dunglass dead?'

They both stared at Gently, but said nothing.

'Well,' Gently said. 'Let's get to what happened. You had this assignation fixed up for last night. You, Mr McGuigan, were waiting at the Stane. Tell me what you saw from up there.'

'I saw you and Miss Merryn,' McGuigan scowled. 'And you picked our very spot, man, for sitting down. And I was cursing you grandly through my beard, I tell you that to your face,'

'Where was your car?' Gently smiled.

'I have a wee hidin'-place in the timber. I was up at the Stane round nine o'clock time – nothing was stirring there then.'

'Did you see Dunglass drive towards Balmagussie?'

'I ken he went off before I got up there.'

'Donnie left at half past eight,' Mary Dunglass said. 'Jamie couldn't have seen him from where he was.'

'So where exactly were you at half past eight?' Gently asked.

McGuigan paused. 'I'd just be setting out from the car,' he said. 'Mary wasn't expecting me till late. I had my supper in Balma'. Then I drove to the place where I leave the car and sat there a while, perhaps half an hour.'

'Could anyone have seen you there, seen you go there?'

'They'd need to know where to look,' McGuigan said. 'I come into the back road out of Glen Skilling, and passed nothing and nobody on the way.'

'That's the opposite end to Halfstarvit?'

'Ay. Dunglass could never have spotted my car.'

'But apparently someone did spot your car – and phoned Mr Dunglass while you were still sitting in it.'

McGuigan stood frowning at the faded carpet. 'I cannot just figure that out,' he said. 'There's never a telephone till you come to Skilling – that's more than four miles away. If the car was seen where I hide it they must have been on the phone in minutes – they'd need a car – and there wasn't a car – I had the road in sight all the time.'

'Was there in fact a phone call?' Gently asked Mary Dunglass.

'Indeed there was,' Mary Dunglass said. 'I heard it ringing, and Donnie picked it up, and straight after that he came to say he was going out.'

'Did you hear what he said?'

'No, I couldn't hear that – he was in the hall, I was in the sitting-room – but at first he sounded angry, then he spoke soft, then he hung up with a good bang. Inspector Blayne was busy tracing the call – maybe he can tell you where it was made from.'

'Hm,' Gently said. 'We'll pass that. Mr McGuigan leaves his car to go up to the Stane. It apparently takes him about half an hour, and presumably he has a private way up there.'

'Och, there's a dozen ways,' McGuigan said. 'If you ken the braes like a mountain man. I took a line up through the trees then worked along to the Stane.'

'Seeing nobody.'

'Just so. And nobody seeing me, you ken. It was a soft, quiet manner of evening, with the doves crooing down below.'

'And at the Stane, nobody.'

'Till yourselves – and I watched ye coming from far away.'

'But Dunglass was up there. He took the path before us. We noticed his tracks on our way up.'

'You did, did you,' McGuigan said, shooting Gently a sharp glance. 'And what time do they say the man died, if I would not be asking a wrong question?'

'Around eleven o'clock, or a little later.'

'Oh my God!' Mary Dunglass exclaimed. She swung away from them, her hands to her face, and gave a little keening moan.

'Then he was well alive,' McGuigan said fiercely, 'when I came down from the Stane last night – and you can give me the time of that yourselves, for you were leaving below when I was leaving above.'

'We saw you at the Stane,' Gently said. 'But when you came down we don't know.'

'I came down then.'

'It's true!' Mary Dunglass cried. 'I met him at the Apron soon after ten.'

'And you came up the path?' Gently said, turning to her.

'Ay, the path – what other way?'

'Then why didn't we see you?'

'Because I saw you first – and I stepped into the trees – and I let you pass!'

'By Heaven,' McGuigan rumbled, 'we're telling you the truth, man – you needn't be setting your springs and traps. Just put a straight question and take a straight answer – the de'il we have to hide from you now.'

Gently hunched a shoulder. 'I'm glad to hear it, because Inspector Blayne will use springs and traps. And if you're to be alibis for one another, it would help if I could place you together by my own witness. Where did we pass you, Mrs Dunglass?'

'It was on the traverse – what we call the Sheepwalk.'

'Do you remember us doing, saying, anything?'

'Ay – the lady slipped – you caught her and kissed her.'

'There's for you, man!' McGuigan chuckled. 'And will you have me say what I keeked at from the Stane?'

'Mr McGuigan,' Brenda said. 'That was quite un-called for and unbecoming a Highland gentleman. But what Mrs Dunglass says is true – I remember a slip coming down.'

'He caught you – he kissed you,' Mary Dunglass said. 'I can't quite recall the words that passed.'

'Thank you,' Brenda said, bowing.

'Ahem!' Gently coughed. 'That seems to answer the question. So we have the two of you placed at the foot of the crag at a little after ten o'clock. Perhaps you'll tell me how long you were there, and if you remember anything unusual happening.'

Mary Dunglass swung away again, and McGuigan's beard set up a few degrees.

'We were there till gey near midnight,' he said shortly. 'And we didna stir from that spot.'

'You heard nothing.'

'No.'

'Dunglass was there.'

'Ay. But spies are quiet bodies.'

'His killer was there.'

'He wouldna be noisy.'

'Dunglass was stabbed.'

'We heard nothing.'

'I – I heard something,' Mary Dunglass faltered. 'I can't say just what or when. It was up the Stane – I thought it might be sheep – I was not minded to regard it just then.'

'You did not tell me!' McGuigan said.

'No, Jamie – I'm sayin' – it was when I was no' minded.'

'There's for you, Mr McGuigan,' Brenda said sweetly. 'You mustn't be pressing when a lady is no' minded.'

'Can you describe the sound?' Gently asked.

'Och no, it was nearly nothing,' Mary Dunglass answered. 'Like a sheep frisking – it could have been that – when they come down thump with their hooves, you ken.' She trembled. 'It wasn't – you don't think—'

'Could you have a shot at placing the time?'

'No – no.' She closed her eyes. 'Oh God – perhaps they're right – about eleven.'

'About eleven.'

She rocked herself, one hand shielding her face from them.

'Dear God, it's terrible,' she said. 'Dear God! At such a time – in that place!'

'Well, we're getting the pattern of it,' Gently said, speaking quickly. 'The murderer was someone who knew about you two. Someone who knew enough to use you as a bait to lure Dunglass up to the Stane. Who knew the braes – that's essential – and knew how to kill a man soundlessly. An active person, almost certainly local, who had a murderous hatred for Dunglass. Doesn't that suggest anyone?'

McGuigan shook his shaggy head. 'I'm at a loss, man, it just baffles me. I can't think who *could* know about us, let alone who would want Dunglass away.'

'Doesn't this bring us back to something else,' Gently said. 'And what Mrs Dunglass was suggesting to Blayne?'

'Oh, that was just a blind!' cried Mary Dunglass. 'I had to tell the man something – I had to steer him off Jamie!'

'Yet it's a fact,' Gently said, 'that your husband quarrelled with the Action Group, and that he was over-deep in their secrets.'

'It was a blind. I knew nothing. It was only to perplex him, give us time!'

McGuigan came striding off the hearth and planted himself in front of Gently.

'Man,' he said, 'ye're plain daft – ye're as glaikit as a lent leveret! What d'ye ken of the Action Group but what yon Blayne body has been feedin' you – and what

114

the lady put him up to, when she would have put him up to anything? D'ye think we're a murderin', assassin-atin' lot – a manner o' Scots I.R.A. – who go planting bombs and slaughterin' innocents – raisin' hell and high water?'

'I think you're handy with guns,' Gently said.

'And what else would ye look for in a Highland deerrun – where the polismen are rare as herrings, an' the English come with trucks and gangs? Man, it's deer we live on here – ye canna raise crops among the heather – an' if I teach the ghillies a wee warfare, who's to cry me blame for that? Keep your English thieves at hame – let honest men rule honest men – and you'll no' hear a gun click in your lug when you come pleasurin' up the glen.'

'Or find a body on the braes?'

'It's none of our work – that's flat! Dunglass could stay or tarry for all the Movement cared or kenned.'

'But still he died.'

'Still he died – with a length o' dirk in his back. And that's an auld Highland custom between men who can't thole one another. Look for a man who hated Dunglass. Look for the tartan Dunglass spat on. But dinna go flisking your wits over the affairs of Egypt – leave the Blayne body to that.'

'Is that a threat?' Gently asked.

'Not a threat – good advice. If I do not point you in the right direction I'm likely to see Barlinnie myself.'

He gave Gently a long, stern stare, his brows knitted, his beard rampant; but then a twinkle began to grow in the blue deep of his eyes.

115

'Man, it's a solemn matter,' he said. 'But I canna let you off in this manner, neither – with me fighting away like an auld fishwife, and you sitting there weighing me up by the pound. Lettie!'

The door opened with surprising briskness and Lettie bobbed into the parlour.

'Lettie – fetch a dram – ye ken the bottle – an' the guid glasses – an' get ane for yourself!'

'Oh Superintendent!' Mary Dunglass cried to Gently. 'You'll be for helping us – you really will?'

'He'll be for it,' Brenda said, jogging her chair across to Mary's. 'Or he'll be for something else. I have him eating out of my hand.'

CHAPTER EIGHT

She was standing upon one of those high precipitous
banks . . . and her tall figure, relieved against the
clear blue sky, seemed almost of supernatural stature.
Guy Mannering, Sir Walter Scott

MCGUIGAN, IN A surge of mountain hospitality,
would now have had them stay for an evening
meal, and promised them a taste of venison such as could
not be had for love nor money in a London hotel. There
was also Knockie trout, a famed variety much esteemed
by Highland gourmets, which the lad Dugald could
obtain at short notice from a trap constructed near the
bridge. Would they not wait and eat with him? Brenda,
who had struck up an understanding with Mary
Dunglass, was inclined to be persuaded; Gently was not.
The Sceptre was fetched. McGuigan reluctantly es-
corted them to it. They drove away, leaving him staring
after them, with Mary Dunglass doll-like at his side.

'Cruel, cruel,' Brenda commented. 'When will we
get such an offer again? And you've hurt Jamie's feelings,

George. He's terribly sensitive. And damn it, I *did* want a go at his venison.'

'So you like him,' Gently grunted. 'He's still a suspect.'

'Good grief – I thought you'd established he *wasn't*!'

Gently shook his head. 'I've established some facts, and watched McGuigan, and listened to him. That's all you can say about that – till something like confirmation turns up.

'Oh, you brain-surgeons,' Brenda groaned. 'Now I know why the police are so hopelessly inadequate. They're just two babes, Jamie and Mary – what confirmation do you need of that?'

'Something a jury will look at twice.'

'Juries are mugs. You must know.'

'So,' Gently said. 'We have to pander to their weakness – with things like evidence, facts.'

'I'm beginning to think,' Brenda said, 'that justice is only a balloon for kids. What really matters is the forensic machinery and whether you fed it the right punch-cards.'

'You're pinching my lines,' Gently said. 'That's what policemen mutter to each other. But if McGuigan and his lady are to buck this one they'll need more holes in their card than they have now.'

'And where do they get them?'

Gently rocked his shoulders. 'We're beginning to shade in our picture of X.'

'Yes – but what chance have strangers like us of recognizing him?'

'Not much,' Gently admitted. 'It'll be up to Blayne.'

They drove on silently. Brenda had a pouty expression and sat drooping low in her seat. The sun was slanting down towards the right and the sky paling to its evening blue. At the end of the long, skeiny glen they joined the Bieth road at Brig o' Shotts, then hustled along, with the sun in their eyes, through Bieth and Ardnadoch to Loch Cray. At Lochcrayhead they had completed a circuit of about one hundred Highland miles, girdling a massif of peaks, streams, Gaelic names and nothing else – except Knockie Lodge.

It was after seven when they reached the cottage. They found Geoffrey and Bridget preparing to set out for dinner. Along the dresser were strung three or four sketches in Geoffrey's full and nervous brushwork. Bridget's knitting had also advanced and sat tidily exhibited on a corner of the table; there was an air of domestic calm about the cottage which contrasted strangely with memories of up-the-glen alarms.

'Oh, good,' Bridget said as they entered. 'We were hoping you'd be back in time to join us. Geoff has booked for four at the Bonnie Strathtudlem. Did you have a nice time?'

Brenda plumped down on the sofa. 'Interesting,' she said. 'You could call it that.'

'Did you go very far?'

'Here and there. Awheel and afoot. We kept it varied.'

'We strolled down to the loch,' Geoffrey said. 'And Bridget took off her shoes and paddled. There's a skiff moored there I'd like to borrow. I did that sketch from the shore of the loch.'

'Nice,' Brenda said. 'Nice. George should try his hand at sketching.'

'Oh, it bores other people,' Geoffrey smiled.

'It wouldn't bore me,' Brenda said.

'I was thinking, tomorrow,' Geoffrey said, 'we could take a picnic up Glen Skilling – Sunday, you know, we don't want to go far – Glen Skilling is just the right distance. Where have you been?'

'Visiting,' Brenda said. 'We met some old friends in Glen Knockie. They wanted to keep us, were rather pressing. But George insisted we shouldn't stay.'

'People do know George,' Bridget said complacently. 'He can't get away from it wherever he goes. Why, he's famous in the village already – somebody left a note for him while we were out.'

'A note?' Gently said.

'Yes – here.' Bridget moved one of Geoffrey's sketches and produced an envelope. 'Somebody pushed it under the door – we don't aspire to a letter-box, as you may have noticed.'

Gently took the envelope. It was of cheap butter-paper, such as one buys in village shops, and was addressed to: The English Policeman Staying At Major Macfarlane's Cottage. Gently slit it carefully with his knife and shook the contents onto the table. A single folded sheet of the same paper fell out. Still using the knife, he unfolded it, then laid the knife on it to hold it flat. It bore a rough drawing of a dirk and the words: *The dirk is never sheathed*.

'Good heavens!' Bridget exclaimed. 'What can *that* mean?'

'Very simple,' Brenda said. 'This afternoon they couldn't shoot George, so this evening they propose to stab him.'

They went to dinner. Gently left Brenda to relate their adventures to Geoffrey and Bridget while he used the Bonnie Strathtudlem's phone to get in touch with Inspector Blayne. Blayne was elusive. Gently reached him at last at The Wild Highlandman in Balmagussie, and then found him very reluctant to agree to a meeting before the morning.

'I've had a long, hard day of it, ye ken,' he grumbled. 'There's maybe not just that urgency about the matter. If it's a case of arrest I'll be right there with ye, but a wee detail or two you can leave with Purdy.'

'It's more than details,' Gently said. 'And you may think it warrants an arrest.'

'Can you give me no hint, man?'

'No,' Gently said. 'There are too many cousins about the place.'

He heard Blayne chuckle. 'Right – right! Perspicacity is one o' the ten virtues – and the brew at the Strathtudlem is no' a bad one – och well, I'll spare the petrol. You'll be at dinner, or I'm mistaken?'

'I'm at dinner,' Gently said.

'Never spoil your digestion, man, for me. I'll be lookin' in about when you're at coffee.'

The Bonnie Strathtudlem's Saturday night dinner involved a haggis of some grease and pungency, served skinning hot with mounds of turnip, cabbage and potatoes mashed with butter. It was preceded by grilled trout, which may or may not have been to Knockie standard, and succeeded by bowls of thick cream laced with stewed cloud-berries and their syrup. The serving was done by two smiling girls and overlooked by the hostess, Mattie Robertson. She was a dark, sturdy woman with a lively eye and emphatic curves. Her lively eye was mostly on Gently and she stationed herself near their table, but Gently had dropped a quiet caution and Mattie heard nothing of cousinly topics. At last she took herself off to a small counter and busied herself brewing coffee.

'She's a beauty,' Brenda said cattily. 'I wouldn't trust her with half a man.'

'I imagine McGuigan has talked to her again,' Gently said. 'She wasn't far away when I was on the phone.'

'Your good looks,' Geoffrey said. 'The lady is a widow, I understand.'

'Men,' Brenda said. 'Why don't they learn?'

'But she can cook,' Geoffrey said.

Brenda made a face.

The coffee was excellent, like the dinner; Mattie Robertson served it herself. She lingered longest pouring for Gently, and somehow managed to spill some in Brenda's saucer.

When Blayne arrived, driving a red Imp loaded with badges and spare lamps, he seemed unwilling to exchange the comforts of the Bonnie Strathtudlem for the cottage. His great nose had a coppery glow, which suggested he hadn't wasted his time at The Wild Highlandman, and the eye he rolled on Mattie Robertson was quite as lively as her own.

'We'll have a dram, man,' he said to Gently. 'You must let the West Perthshire buy you a drink. Ay, we're on business, I ken that, but it'll go better with a wet whistle.'

The dram became two drams when the resident accordionist threw off a strathspey, and Blayne's large feet thumped the floor and his glass waved and slopped aloft. Then he led a chorus of 'Down In The Glen' in a strong and unctuous tenor, and whooped and spun himself round with the others after the final clashing chord. At last Gently edged him through the door, and with Brenda, led him gangling down the street.

'Och, it does no harm, man,' he vociferated. 'You canna always be in the saddle – a polisman should mix wi' people, you ken that – an' that Mrs Robertson is a braw woman.'

'I hope you're single, Inspector,' Brenda said archly.

'Oh, ay, I'm much o' that category, Miss Merryn. An' though I'm a member of such a sober calling – she's a braw woman, and I've often thought so.'

But when he was sat down in the cool of the cottage, Blayne seemed to cast his vapours from him. He listened solemnly to their account of what happened in Glen Knockie, and showed real concern when he saw Gently's letter.

'The wuddie idiots!' he exclaimed. 'Have they no respect for a man o' your standin'? Lockin' you away in gamecupboards – shootin' at you – and sendin' you threatenin' letters too! A fine account of us you'll be takin' back to the great men in Whitehall – leave alone the publicity here. You'll be for pressin' charges, of course?'

Gently shook his head. 'McGuigan offered us

satisfaction, and we accepted it. I think his men made a genuine mistake. Apparently they need to be vigilant up Glen Knockie.'

'That may be – but shootin' at you! And now this ugly sort of missive.'

'The letter,' Gently said, 'belongs to a different department. It couldn't have originated in Glen Knockie.'

'You're sure o' that, man?'

'Pretty sure. It was delivered about the time we were talking to McGuigan. The nearest phone is at Brigg o' Shotts, and the distance and times would make it impossible. Also, the writer of the letter didn't seem to know my name, which the Knockie people certainly did. No: the letter originated right here – with someone who didn't like me talking to you.'

'Wi' the murderer, you're sayin',' Blayne said.

'With the murderer or murderers,' Gently said. 'With someone who saw me on the braes last night – and saw me visit you this morning. On the face of it this letter exonerates McGuigan by the simple fact that he couldn't have sent it, but if there are those who are watching his interest then that line of reasoning doesn't apply.'

Blayne sucked in his cheeks. 'Is that what you're thinkin'?'

'I'm not sure,' Gently said, 'what I'm thinking. I'm inclined to believe McGuigan's story, and the letter helps, though it isn't proof.'

'He might have arranged for it earlier,' Blayne suggested. 'When he was in touch with Mattie Robertson, God help us!'

'It isn't his style,' Gently said, frowning. 'Neither the letter itself nor the extravagant manner. What it suggests is fanaticism – hate – unbalance – a strain of puerility. That isn't McGuigan. But it sounds very like a person who would plot to stab a man in the back. Have you no ideas?'

'De'il a one,' Blayne said. 'I cannot raise a prospect, man. I've a pretty guid picture now o' Donnie's acquaintance, but there's never a one you can tie in with this.'

'Mrs Dunglass mentioned a woman he was seeing in Balmagussie.'

Blayne grinned. 'Ay – Poppy Frazer. I was havin' a crack with her this afternoon. She's, ah – beggin' Miss Merryn's pardon – one o' the quality circuit from Glasgow. Dunglass fetched her up here some weeks since – he's no' much use to Poppy dead.'

'Had he any other connections with women?'

'Nave I've heard of up to date. But Donnie was a canny laddie, that I'm learnin'. He's not easy to back-track on.'

'So,' Gently said. 'No other prospects – it lies between McGuigan and you-know-who. I don't like McGuigan, you don't like the others – and McGuigan agrees with you up to the hilt.'

'It's a deeficult situation,' Blayne said, working his shoulders. 'I ken you're for McGuigan, in spite o' his sodjers.'

'I'm for him too,' Brenda said. 'Though you can hang his sodjers from the next tree.'

'Still – I canna quite overlook that mannie – and fine

125

the Superintendent kens my position – I'll be for a session or two wi' Mr McGuigan – and for clearin' up the lady's lees.'

'That's understood,' Gently said.

'Ay – and as for the other, I've no done wi' that. An' you'll give me credit I'll have words wi' McGuigan touchin' the impropriety of private militia. But – when all's said and done – there's not much to go on save the lady's haverings and maybe the weapon. And on the other hand there's motive and opportunity – which are powerful factors in court decisions. Och, it's just the way I was tellin' you this mornin'. There'll be small credit in it for Alistair Blayne.'

'Tell me something,' Gently said. 'Did you trace that call Dunglass received?'

'The call – ay,' Blayne said slowly. 'In a manner o' speakin' we did that. One o' the Forestry boxes had been tampered with – there's two, you ken, along the braes – the lock was forced with a knife or the like. McMorris, the ranger, drew our attention to it.'

'Where is that box?'

'At the Skilling end – no' far from where McGuigan would have left his car.'

'Is there a record of the call?'

'Just a local call. We have the misfortune to be automatic up to Lochcrayhead.'

'When was it timed?'

'At 8.22. I'm thinkin' there's small doubt it was the call to Dunglass. And to anticipate the natural curiosity of a man like yourself – ay, we have a braw set o' dabs off the instrument.'

'Do you know them?' Gently asked.

Blayne wagged his head. 'You'd not expect them to be on record. But we have them – and soon we'll have Mr McGuigan's – and comparin' the two will be vastly informative.'

'Oh, what nonsense!' Brenda exclaimed. 'You can't suspect Jamie of making that call.'

'I didn't exactly say I did, Miss Merryn,' Blayne said. 'But there'll be proof goin' there of one way or the other. If the dabs do not match we ken fine there was another body about the braes – an' if they do, well, they do, and Mr McGuigan must tell us why.'

'But meanwhile,' Gently said, 'there's another comparison you can make.'

'Which is that?'

'Between the dabs on the phone – and any dabs you can find on this letter.'

'Ay,' Blayne said, pausing and hollowing his cheeks. 'That's true – very true. A match there would be full of interest.'

'In my book it would mean almost certainly that the owner of the dabs was the murderer.'

'I ken that – I ken that. The mannie was very rash wi' his letter.'

He stared for some moments at the letter, which still lay weighted with Gently's knife; then, using the knife, he folded the sheet and juggled it back into its envelope.

'I don't need to ask – you didn't touch it?'

'Not the sheet,' Gently said. 'The envelope was handled.'

'Then I'll just away back with it to Balma' and give

it the benefit o' Purdy's science. You'll be wanting to know the result, I'm thinkin'.'

'Yes,' Gently said. 'Ring me at the Bonnie Strathtud-lem.'

'The Bonnie Strathtudlem.' Blayne's face twisted. 'I nearly forgot – I must talk to the lady.' He sighed, tucking the envelope into a shabby wallet. 'This is not an auspicious occasion,' he said. 'You cannot well make a right impression by pokin' into a lady's private business. An' Mattie Robertson – I don't ken – she's as handsome a female as the next. I'd sooner be callin' her to a private interview on some other subject than bloody murder.'

They accompanied Blayne back to the Bonnie Strath-tudlem and watched him accost the handsome Mrs Robertson, then Gently proposed a walk up the back road to look for the spot where McGuigan had parked. The bar was crowding with Saturday trade, so Bridget graciously gave her consent, and the four of them set out across the bridge and turned right towards Glen Skilling.

They passed the Lodge, where a glimpse of a blue Sunbeam Alpine indicated the return of Mary Dunglass from Glen Knockie, and soon were climbing a steady gradient through silent stands of oak and ash. Rightward the trees were spaced thinly, giving some views across the strath, but leftward, where they climbed the braes, they were densely massed and filled between with hazel bush. There was an air of moistness and growth. All along the track small rivulets were crossing and flooding the hollows. Huge black slugs, mostly in pairs, were gliding confidently on the wet surfaces. At length the road levelled out, while at the same time becoming rougher and muddier; and began to display that penchant for endlessness which is the hallmark of Highland roads.

'Must we go on *much* farther,' Bridget wanted to know. 'There really is a great deal of sameness about it. And I don't think George knows what he's looking for anyway – and I'm certain he won't find it.'

'Bear up, old dear,' Geoffrey said. 'It's only five miles to Glen Skilling.'

'But I didn't offer to walk to Glen Skilling,' Bridget said. 'And if it's only five miles, we've probably passed it.'

'I think we can't be far off now,' Gently said. 'What we're looking for is a gate or driveway – anywhere you could run a car in out of sight. We know it isn't very far from the road.'

They turned a bend by a big outcrop and the twilight of the trees suddenly lightened. A short distance ahead they could see a great crag slanting up nakedly from the track. The trees hung back from it; to the side of the crag was a steep incline of crumbled rock. It seemed to flow out from behind a low rockrim that guarded the flank of the crag.

'Aha!' Gently said. 'This could be it.'

He hurried up the incline to peer behind the rockrim. It concealed a space about twenty feet long with a floor of thin, fawny turf. The rockrim was only a few feet high but it was a yard or two in width. A car, placed carefully behind it, would be invisible from the road.

'But could he have got it up here?' Brenda queried, joining Gently. 'I'm darned if I'll try it with my *1100*.'

'Oh yes, he got it up here,' Gently said, pointing to some oil spots. 'And he's right about the road – you can see it through that crevice.'

'So what do we know now?'

'We know McGuigan was telling us the truth about this. But what I'd like to know is where the person was hidden who shopped McGuigan to Dunglass.'

He stared about the spot. The flank of the crag merged precipitously into the trees, which, with their stockades of blunt-leaved hazels, presented an unbroken and close-knit front. The road was hemmed by a similar screen, and was here a short stretch between sharp bends. There was no indication of an entry having been forced through the skirts of the trees.

'He'd have to be in there somewhere,' Brenda ventured.

Gently shook his head. 'It doesn't seem likely. He'd have to be too close if he was to see anything, and he couldn't have got away again without some noise. It would help if we knew where that Forestry box was.'

'Why don't you ask the lady?' Bridget said.

'What lady?' Gently asked, turning.

'The lady who's watching us – up there!'

They looked where she was pointing. Above the crag, where it rounded off into the brae, a tall girl with a large dog stood silhouetted against the sky. She was dressed in faded jeans and a sloppy sweater and lounged there with an easy, masculine negligence. She was looking down at them scornfully, her tanned face framed by short, bushy hair.

'Glory!' Brenda whispered. 'She'll be the original mountain hizzie.'

'That's your question answered, George,' Geoffrey murmured. 'The one above sees all.'

'I wonder if she bites,' Brenda whispered. 'The way she's looking at us I think she would. She's taken against us, that's plain. We're just four more slugs in her evening landscape.'

The girl now drew herself up stiffly and took two steps nearer the edge.

'D'ye hear me, down there!' she called, her voice echoing and sharply clear.

'We hear you,' Gently called back. 'Please, can you tell us where the Forestry keeps its phone-box?'

'Ay I can,' her voice rang down. 'But you're no' a Forestryman, southron. Gae hame – gae home, that's a' I've to tell ye – we need no English up the glens. Take your bonnie leddies an' your braw cars and point them south. Gae hame!'

'Somebody should warn MacBraynes,' Brenda said. 'This female will ruin the tourist trade.'

'Wait!' Gently called. 'What's your name?'

The girl threw back her head and laughed. 'Ye ken I'm Scots, I ken you're English – that's a' the introduction needed. An' ye hear me tell you – Scots to English – awa', back to the land o' the serpent!'

Then she spoke a word to the dog, and the two of them turned and moved away. In a moment they had jumped down into some hollow and disappeared from view.

'Well!' exclaimed Bridget indignantly. 'If *that's* all the Scots think of us!'

'I get the impression she was a shade ultra,' Geoffrey said. 'I imagine she was one of the silver dirk brigade, George.'

'She's a nut-case,' Brenda said. 'She was aaacting her uncombed head off. Really, someone should civilize these wild Highlanders.'

Gently stared at the vacant crag. 'Yes,' he said.

CHAPTER NINE

If you don't know the course, follow *Madie*.
                                    Yacht Club proverb

BLAYNE HAD RUNG back shortly before closing time to tell Gently the dabs matched, and Gently had smoked a silent pipe over this information before turning in along with Geoffrey. He slept poorly. Geoffrey snored, and Gently was troubled by a recurring dream. In this dream he was clinging to a perpendicular rockface, with nothing but a glassy surface above him. Below him, with dirks clutched between their teeth, climbed Hamish, Dugald and the 'Sons of Ivor', while the sweater-girl with her slavering wolf-hound urged them on from a convenient eminence. At the foot of the rock-face stood Blayne, McGuigan, Mary Dunglass and Mattie Robertson, drinking whisky from cut-glass tumblers and speculating if he would fall or be cut to pieces. In effect, Gently fell, because the rockface always concluded by tilting outwards, and he descended sickeningly to find his bed thrusting up into his back. It was an unpleasant dream. Each time he woke with sweat standing on his brow. Though he knew how it would end, the relief of the knowledge was always witheld till the waking moment.

He rose in the morning feeling dull-eyed and staring sourly at the new-made sunlight. Bridget was already bustling about preparing the picnic they were to take up Glen Skilling. Mrs McFie, dressed in a sepulchral two-piece and a ruffled blouse, and smelling of lavender, seemed almost snappish as she got the breakfast, perhaps due to her early-kirk attendance. Gently ventured an inquiry about the sweater-girl, but Mrs McFie was determinedly unhelpful. She kent one or two o' that description, she said, but apparently little in their favour.

'They're a sinful an' scornful generation, Mr Gently, wi' their indecent clothes an' clarty habits – they'll come to no guid – the Buik has a word for 'em – I'm glad to report there are none in Tudlem.'

'This one was very tall,' Gently persisted. 'She was taller than most men.'

'That would be no disteenction,' Mrs McFie said. 'They come lang an' rough about the hills. There's Jeanie Dinwhiddy – she's a lang ane – but she's up to no guid down in Glesca. An' Meg Macready – she'd suit – but she wouldna be rovin' the braes with a dog. No, I canna just say exactly who your fleerin' lassie would be, but this I'll give ye for Gospel truth – she was na at the kirk this mornin'.'

'Which surprises me,' Brenda put in. 'Because she had a pulpiteering manner.'

'No doubt,' Mrs McFie said. 'But it wasna contracted by huggin' a pew.'

When she'd gone – the Major, she told them, expected no washing-up from her on the Sabbath – Gently watched for a while as Bridget cut neat, slim ham-and-tongue sandwiches. Then he sighed and knocked out his pipe.

'I'll have to take a rain-check on that,' he said.

'You'll have to what?' Bridget said, glaring.

'I'm sorry. I've figured a fresh angle on the Dunglass business.'

'A fresh angle! But it isn't your case.'

'I know,' Gently said. 'But I'm in it all the same. And because I'm in it I can't stop thinking about it, and when I think about it I come up with angles.'

'Oh, my goodness!' Bridget groaned. 'Why does one ever go on holiday with this man? George, I've cut your sandwiches, and that's that – you're coming on this picnic, and you're going to like it.'

Gently shook his head. 'Sorry, Bridgie. The angle I've figured won't wait.'

'Then tell it to Blayne!'

'Blayne might not appreciate it. And he might not handle it right if he did.'

'May we know what it is?' Geoffrey inquired from the kitchen, where he was wiping while Brenda washed. 'I've been giving the case some thought myself, but I haven't come up with anything bright.'

'This,' Gently said, 'is just a . . . hunch. It may mean only my wasting a day. But when you put a ferret in one end of a burrow it's usually worth watching what comes out the other.'

135

'Go on,' Geoffrey said. 'It sounds promising.'

'Blayne is the ferret,' Gently said. 'He'll be going into Knockie first thing this morning and showing his sharp little teeth to McGuigan. I don't think he'll arrest him – not now, after those two sets of dabs checked out; but if he's worth his salt he'll make McGuigan believe he's in imminent danger of being arrested.'

'You don't think McGuigan will bolt,' Geoffrey said.

'No,' Gently said. 'He'll hardly do that. But he won't sit pat either and wait for Blayne to arrest him. He'll do some hard thinking – perhaps make a move. McGuigan knows the set-up. He can guess better than anyone who could have been involved in killing Dunglass. If it's a Nationalist affair he may not want to divulge it, but he can't afford not to be able to.'

'Subtle,' Geoffrey said. 'So he could lead you to the murderer.'

'He'll follow his hunches, no doubt,' Gently shrugged.

'And you want to watch him.'

'I want to watch him. If anyone knows where to look it's McGuigan.'

Brenda came out of the kitchen, stood leaning, looking. 'Ah well,' she sighed. 'Don't grieve for me, Bridget. I'm beginning to get the hang of being George's girl-friend.'

'I've said it before,' Bridget said. 'And I'll probably be saying it all my life – he's the most infuriating of men.'

'One day I'll tame him,' Brenda assured her.

It was a long time since Gently had last been employed on a stake-out, and he went about the details of this one

136

with a boyish sort of pleasure. First, he needed a fresh car, the Sceptre by now being too well-known. Geoffrey offered him the Hawk, but Gently turned it down on the grounds that people always look twice at a large car. Instead, he visited the garage across the road, where they offered him a Series V Minx – not perhaps the car of all others for shadowing a hot Cortina, but ideally inconspicuous in the Hillman-minded Highlands.

'I'm expecting a friend to drop in,' Gently lied to the garage-proprietor. 'He's on a cycling tour. We're leaving a car behind so he can drive out to join us up Glen Skilling.'

'Ay, an' a braw day for ye, too,' the man replied unsuspiciously. 'Ye winna see a finer sight than the Braes o' Skilling in June.'

So the Minx was chartered and fuelled and drifted back to the cottage. Bridget's picnic was divided in two and one half packed in the Minx's boot. Then, at Gently's instance, the Minx and the Hawk set off together, and paused at the store to buy chocolate and spread the gospel of the cyclist and the picnic.

'So much for the cousins,' Gently grinned, as the two cars continued in convoy out of the village. 'That should take care of any message going Knockie-way. All we have to worry about now is that sheep-farmer on the track, but we're hardly likely to run into his confounded sheep again.'

'What about the boy-soldier,' Brenda said. 'How do we know he won't be up there.'

'We don't,' Gently said. 'But I think it's unlikely – after Blayne has done his job. I think the Knockie

Irregulars will be lying low, and that goes for their sentry too. A proper Sabbath peace and calm will be the order of the day at Knockie.'

'Well, I think it's daft,' Brenda said. 'But I don't mind picnicking there alone with you.'

'We'll get that out of it at all events,' Gently smiled. 'And one can do worse than Knockie Forest.'

They arrived at the junction of the Skilling Road. Geoffrey slowed, waved and turned off. The Minx pressed on at an easy-breathed sixty along the route they had followed the day before. They were finding more traffic today, probably excursionists from Glasgow, Edinburgh, Stirling, Perth, but Gently weaved by it confidently and slid the long miles swiftly away. The Minx was kin to the Sceptre and came familiarly to his hand. It went sure-footed into bends and pulled strongly on the steep gradients.

By ten they reached Torlinnhead and the turn to the track over the tops. In his wisdom, Gently engaged first for the initial scramble, and the Minx clambered up it uncomplaining. In sight of the farm he halted briefly to reconnoitre from a bank, but the sheep were visible on a distant pasture and the farmhouse apparently deserted. They went by it. Nobody stared. The Minx chuntered sturdily on its way. Within half an hour they were over the tops and approaching the spot where the Sceptre had been bogged.

'Now we just make the car invisible,' Brenda said. 'That shouldn't trouble the trained brain.'

'If McGuigan can do it at Tudlem,' Gently chuckled 'we should be able to do it at Knockie. See over there.'

He pointed to some boulders that stood in a group to the left of the track. A declivity resembling the dry bed of a stream made a line towards and behind them. Gently stopped and got out to explore. The ground was rough but free from gullies. He returned to the Minx, drove it cautiously to the declivity, turned it, backed it behind the boulders. Then he checked the effectiveness of the concealment from the track. Nothing showed. The Minx was swallowed up in the scattered vastness of the tops.

'And now we just sit here,' Brenda said. 'Making non-noises like policemen.'

'Not exactly,' Gently grinned. 'Because McGuigan may leave by the other way. I don't think he will. Mary Dunglass used the track when she wanted to get here unobserved, and I imagine it's McGuigan's quiet way out. But we can't rely on that.'

'Then I take it we're going to play boy-soldiers.'

'Something of that sort,' Gently said. 'I'd say Dugald had a hideaway on the brow of the ridge there. We probably shan't do better than follow his example.'

He collected the picnic from the boot, Brenda carried the glasses, and they made their way through the boulders and heather. The ridge slanted upwards for a short distance then levelled off in flats and hollows. It was a perfect spot for observation. The track ran immediately below it. Beyond was the vista of the top of the glen with the Lodge a miniature among its trees. In the other direction the tops and the track spread into a distance of sun-hazed peaks, and by lying in a hollow one could watch all this without being in view from any part of it.

Gently picked his hollow, took the glasses, sprawled on his elbows and surveyed the Lodge.

'We've timed it nicely,' he said. 'Blayne is still there. That's a police Super Snipe in the courtyard.'

'Any chocolate soldiers around?'

'There's someone by the stream with a rod or a net.'

'Probably the boy-soldier after trout,' Brenda said, slumping down happily. 'That's Menace No. 1 taken care of. We can relax, go loose.'

'Not so loose,' Gently said, 'that we can't jump into action fast if need be.'

'Nuts,' Brenda said. 'This is a game, remember? You're only in it for the kicks.'

She spread herself lazily on the scant heather, closed her eyes, basked. The sun bored down from a Wedgwood sky. A faint, aromatic breeze sissed through the heather. Other than this sound the tops were silent with a massive, sidereal silence, so that one might have been suspended in space and insensibly travelling among the stars. There were no birds, apparently no animals, not even a bee or a scampering ant. Just the breeze and the kissing sun and the still pressure of rock and heather.

Gently lowered the glasses and lit his pipe. There was no telling how long Blayne had been at the Lodge. It was on the cards he'd first visited Mary Dunglass and was only now beginning his session with McGuigan. And somehow Gently's hunch, which had seemed so probable when he was developing it to Geoffrey, up here began to seem less likely, wore more the aspect of chairborne theorizing. Blayne was not playing a game. Though he might not arrest McGuigan, he had grounds for pulling him in and making him sweat: for keeping him for hours in some sordid little room and playing all the interrogator's tricks on him. Then again, McGuigan, if left at liberty, might only fly straight to a lawyer or Mary Dunglass. It might be some little time before he pulled himself together and took independent action – if he ever did. No: Gently's hunch was full of loopholes through which the breeze of the tops blew gaily. Better face it. He was playing a long one. As Brenda said, it was for the kicks.

'You're thinking,' Brenda said, her eyes shut. 'I can feel you thinking. Don't do it.'

'Perhaps I'm thinking about you,' Gently smiled.

'No you're not,' Brenda said. 'I'd feel that too.'

'Well, I'm thinking about you now,' Gently said.

'That's better,' Brenda said. 'Keep doing that. I'm what's important up here, George Gently, not what's o'clock with the hairy lairdies.'

'Do you ever get sunburned?' Gently asked.

'Ugh,' Brenda said. 'To hell with sunburn. Put that pipe away and stop making noises. Just fill in time like an irrational being.'

Blayne departed at half-past twelve, not taking McGuigan along with him. Gently watched the lanky Inspector and the solid Purdy stand talking some moments before getting in their car. Nothing else of note had happened down at the Lodge. Somebody had washed the Land Rover in the courtyard. Dugald, if it was he, had returned from his fishing; that was the sum total of activity.

'And now they'll have lunch,' Brenda said. 'Jamie

won't miss that for a dozen Blaynes. So we'll just leave them to get on with their venison while we tackle Bridget's sandwiches.'

She spread a picnic cloth, and they ate, Gently with his eye continually on the house. But his hunch seemed to be growing particularly faint over that domestic little meal. The stake-out accompanied by a picnic was fast becoming a simple picnic, and the green Minx lurking behind the boulders was assuming a faintly mocking air.

Blayne had been, Blayne had gone, but no rabbit was bolting out of Glen Knockie . . .

'We'll give him till three,' Gently said glumly, draining the last of the Thermos tea.

'I don't mind, really,' Brenda said. 'I'm getting a rest in. I like it here.'

'But it's boring, staying in one spot, however spectacular the scenery. And we're on holiday or something. And I'm just making an ass of myself.'

Brenda hitched up on one elbow. 'George,' she said, 'you're an old idiot. Being here makes perfect sense, and we're jolly well stopping here till Jamie shows.'

'We could wait all day.'

'So we'll wait. It's what I expected when I came along.'

'I may have misjudged McGuigan . . .'

'Then that makes two of us. Just you get back to watching the house.'

Gently shrugged and did as she bid him, and Brenda repacked the picnic. It was barely done when he gave an exclamation and motioned to Brenda to slide up beside him.

'Who is it – Jamie?'

'Yes. He's just gone across to the coach-house.'

'Now who's making an ass of himself!'

'It doesn't mean to say he's fetching his car.'

But McGuigan was fetching his car. They saw the blue Cortina slide out of the coach-house, vanish into the trees, re-appear, stop at the gate across the track.

'Come on!' Gently exclaimed, grabbing the picnic basket. 'We've got to get out of here ahead of him.'

'Ahead of him? Why?'

'Because if we follow him we'll probably lose him at the other end.'

Till that moment he hadn't seen it, but now he saw it very plainly. On that bare track they would need to lag perhaps half a mile behind their quarry. There could be no closing up till they were well past the farm, and the difficult descent at the end would delay them till McGuigan was clear away. At Torlinnhead, he had the choice of turning east or west.

'Get in quick!'

Gently jammed down the pedal and the Minx started first bang. He sent it pitching across the rough top and thudding down on to the track. He drove recklessly. The Minx had a rugged suspension and didn't flinch. It pounded along at a flickering forty and sailed through the potholes without bottoming. In his mirror he watched the track ribboning away to its vanishing point by the ridge, then swing across and vanish behind the sudden lift of an out-crop.

'Was there any sign of him?'

'No,' Brenda said. 'Take it easy. This isn't Brands Hatch.'

'He may have been bluffing.'

'Like why would he do that?'

'Somebody may have caught a flash from the glasses.'

'Oh, for Heaven's sake,' Brenda said. 'What reason would he have to think we were watching him?'

'Not us – Blayne's men,' Gently said. 'If I'd been Blayne I'd have had some up here.'

He drove the next straight stretch uncomfortably fast then halted the car in the dip beyond. He jumped out, ran back, stood peering from behind a rock. Then he dashed back to the car. He was grinning.

'Right – we've hooked him,' he said. 'He's coming along nice and quietly. I don't think he suspects a thing.'

'Of course, he may have bluffed you after all,' Brenda said spitefully. 'You don't *know* it's McGuigan driving the Cortina.'

'Actually, I do love you,' Gently grinned.

'Ah,' Brenda said. 'Well, I could be wrong.'

Gently dropped the speed, but still pressed on at a rate he judged was faster than McGuigan's. The Minx grumbled along sturdily, obviously at home in this sort of country. They passed the farm again without apparently attracting attention, moaned and slithered down the descent, came to the barn at the bottom. Here Gently twisted and dug with the Minx and at last screwed it backwards into the barn. The barn was dark. Unless McGuigan were specially watching for it he would scarcely notice a car in there.

'It seems terribly mean,' Brenda mused. 'The poor

angel just doesn't have a chance. He comes blithely along, all innocence, never dreaming he's being played cat-and-mouse with. Don't you ever feel it's unsporting, George?'

'It doesn't happen to be a sport,' Gently said. 'And McGuigan's innocence is far from proven. Otherwise we wouldn't be here.'

'Still, I *feel* mean,' Brenda said. 'I feel we ought to give McGuigan a toot. Just to show there's no ill-feeling.'

'Hush,' Gently said. 'Here he comes.'

The blue Cortina buzzed cautiously by them, and the last doubt was answered: McGuigan was driving it. His beard and straight arms swept past at a few yards distance. Gently listened, heard the engine dull as McGuigan paused at the junction; then he started the Minx and rolled out of the barn and purred quietly after the Cortina.

The Cortina had turned right.

'Not to Strathtudlem,' Gently muttered.

'It's the Logie road,' Brenda said. 'What can he be wanting down there?'

'It connects with the A9,' Gently said. 'Inverness and points north.'

'What's at Inverness?'

Gently shrugged, settled the Minx at a comfortable distance behind the Cortina.

McGuigan was driving at a modest fifty, which suggested he hadn't spotted his tail. It also suggested to Gently that McGuigan's trip would probably be a short one. A hundred, two hundred miles and McGuigan would have been flogging his steed. The GT was built to travel fast and McGuigan had shown he liked it that way. Yet short or long, a trip on this road was leading them further away from the Strathtudlem area. Could it just be that McGuigan really was wise to them, had some reason for drawing them off on a goose-hunt?

They drove three miles, came to a left-hand junction with signpost beside it. McGuigan's winker went and he ducked down off the main road. The signpost said: GLENNY ½, and the road it indicated was narrow but beautifully surfaced and maintained. It snaked through a stand of very tall oaks beyond and above which rose shaggy braes.

'Map,' Gently said, making the turn.

Brenda hastily unfolded the map.

'It's a cul-de-sac,' she said. 'Quite short. Leads to a big house – McClune Castle.'

'A castle,' Gently said, easing. 'That'll be the one you can see from the track. It's quite a place. I wonder who lives there.'

'We're sure to find out,' Brenda groaned. 'And the wrong way.'

The road made two sweeping turns and arrived suddenly at a big arched gateway. Beyond the gateway, across wide lawns, rose the turreted splendour of a castellated house. The blue Cortina was driving straight towards it. They watched it park in front of the portico. McGuigan got out, ran up the steps and passed straight through the doors, which stood open. Nobody questioned his going in. Nobody stirred about the grounds.

CHAPTER TEN

Though right be aft put down by strength,
  As mony a day we saw that,
The true and leilfu' cause at length
  Shall bear the grie for a' that.
  'A New Song To An Old Tune', Sir Walter Scott

McCLUNE CASTLE WAS no lightweight. It had been conceived in the grandest style of Baronial Scottish, with massive pepperpot towers, groves of pointed windows and an irregular forest of perching turrets. It was also very meticulously maintained. The windows glinted, the lawns was precisely cut and edged, the sweep of blue granite chippings were raked and weedless and the ornate gates were newly leathered. Besides McGuigan's Cortina, there stood on the sweep a glittering maroon Silver Shadow.

'Ah, money,' Brenda breathed. 'And I thought they were so hard up in Scotland.'

'Money and consequence,' Gently said. 'But what has McGuigan to do with either?'

'Well, he was pretty familiar with it,' Brenda said. 'The way he drifted up there and sailed in. Perhaps he's a cousin thirty-six times removed. Or flogs his venison to Lord Muck.'

Gently shook his head, staring, running his eye all round the castle. Tradesmen and thirty-sixth cousins would scarcely bowl in there unannounced. Who was this McGuigan had run to when he felt the law beginning to lean on him – if that was the reason he had come here? Who would he know as well as that . . . ?

'So what now?' Brenda asked. 'The nearest phone-box, and ring Blayne?'

'Not so quick,' Gently said. 'I'd like to know what's going on there.'

'Marvellous. Do we breeze in like Jamie?'

'It might be worth trying,' Gently grinned. 'But I'd like to make it inconspicuous. And the trees do come in close at the side of the house.'

'Yes, we could climb them,' Brenda said. 'Then come in swinging, Tarzan-fashion. Only first we have to reach them.'

'So,' Gently said. 'We'd better see where the road here takes us.'

He set the Minx rolling again, past the gates, into more trees. Beyond the gates it was less well surfaced and seemed likely to degenerate into a track. But it continued in a respectable way, bearing always to the right, till it had apparently circumnavigated that side of the grounds and they arrived at a less splendid pair of gates.

'The tradesman's entrance,' Brenda said. 'We could pretend to be insurance salesmen.'

'Tchk,' Gently said. 'Not on the Sabbath. And there be dragons that way in any case.'

He indicated a lodge-house and a terrace of half a dozen neat cottages. Smoke was climbing from one or two of the chimney and a mongrel dog squatted with a bone in the driveway. As they paused, watching, a small girl came trotting from the cottages to stare back at them. She wore a knitted jersey that reached half-way down her hips, a radiant smile, and nothing else.

'That's the way to bring them up,' Brenda said. 'Plenty of fresh air and Andrew Carnegie. Do you think she could tell us who the Super-Laird is?'

'Probably,' Gently said. 'But we won't trouble her.'

'Ah,' Brenda sighed. 'If Mary Quant could see this lassie. She'd surely sweep the board at Melbourne.'

Gently drove on. The road now no longer made any pretension to a surface, and they were bumbling again over naked rock with rashes of chippings and black mud. They were climbing, too, wriggling their way up into the moist, still trees; but still, by Gently's computation, describing a circle about the castle. Then the track ended. It had brought them to a small, stone, Gothic pavilion. The pavilion stood in a clearing. It faced directly down at the castle.

Gently parked the Minx and they got out. He levelled the glasses at the castle. On this side the curtain wall between the towers was pierced by a range of sash windows. An ornate fountain on the lawn was sending up a triple rainbow spray and behind the fountain tall french doors stood folded back above shallow steps.

'Very pretty,' Brenda said. 'But I don't see it gets us anywhere.'

'Take these,' Gently said, handing her the glasses. 'Concentrate on what you can see through the doors.'

Brenda looked.

'Aha – Jamie! He's got his beard up at another gentleman.'

'Gesturing, waving his arms, isn't he?'

'Doing just that,' Brenda agreed.

'Appealing to the other gentleman,' Gently said. 'Arguing, wanting him to do something. Now I wonder what it could be – and why the other gentleman is in a position to do it.'

Brenda lowered the glasses, stared at him.

'Are you thinking what I'm thinking?' she said. 'What are you thinking?'

'About the Affairs of Egypt – and – what was he called? The Lord Thistle.'

Gently nodded slowly. 'The Lord Thistle – the grand Chieftain of the Chieftains. Who else would McGuigan go to see if the Dunglass murder were a Nationalist business? And it fits. It accounts for the way he drove up here and went straight in. He's one of the top Nationalists himself and he'd certainly have direct access to the leader.'

'Then – the murder *is* a Nationalist job?'

'It's beginning to look very much that way.'

'And Jamie and Mary are in the clear.'

'Not quite yet,' Gently said. 'Not quite yet.' He took the glasses and stared again at the tantlizing tableau beyond the doors. But it was just too far away for him to exercise his talent for lip-reading. McGuigan was still sawing away, the other man straight, motionless, listening. He was slighter than McGuigan, though still tall, with dark hair cut short.

Gently lowered the glasses. 'It's no good,' he said. 'We'll just have to get in a bit closer.'

'We can't,' Brenda said. 'They're bound to spot us.'

'We can get down here to the edge of the trees.'

'But you couldn't hear them from there.'

'Let's go,' Gently said. 'Perhaps we can work something else when we get there.'

'I'll bet we can,' Brenda said. 'And it won't be a game-store this time. There'll be a deep, dank dungeon in that castle, and that's where our skeletons will be found.'

In fact there was a regular path from the pavilion leading down to the lawns. It dived under the gloomy cover of a rhododendron thicket which waved bright blossom high above them. It proceeded downwards with stone-flagged steps to a wrought-iron gate facing the fountain. The gate was flanked by wistaria trees. The trees offered just the right amount of cover.

'Now,' Gently said, raising his glasses. But again he was disappointed. He found McGuigan standing with his back to him and the other man retiring into the room. The other man went on his knees. He was fiddling with something. Gently suddenly realized the something was a safe. Its door swung open, the man reached inside, came up carrying a blue-bound folio.

'Glory!' Brenda breathed. 'Another bluebook. And I can see the dirk on it from here.'

'And it isn't minutes this time,' Gently muttered. 'McGuigan wasn't doing his top to consult those.'

The dark-haired man, whose sharp features they could now distinguish for the first time, ran down a thumb-index on the folio, opened and consulted it. He read something from it to McGuigan, but with his face at an angle from Gently, then closed it and laid it on a table. McGuigan had reacted with a fierce snatch of his head. 'And that's all?' the dark-haired man's lips said. 'Ay, it's enough,' McGuigan's lips replied. 'I don't have to warn you, Jamie,' the dark-haired man's lips said, then he put his hand on McGuigan's shoulder and accompanied him towards an inner door.

'Quick!' Gently exclaimed. 'Round to the front. Keep them busy there for five minutes.'

'But what shall I do!' Brenda wailed.

'Scream – break windows – strip – anything!'

'Oh my God,' Brenda wailed. 'This is the last time – ever!'

But she darted through the gate and across the lawn and round the blind bastion of the corner tower. Gently hung on a moment. For a short space the peace of McClune Castle proceeded, then a car-door slammed, an engine pealed, chippings rattled and there came a shout of anger.

'Good girl!' Gently grinned. He raced over the lawn and through the french doors. The blue folio was lying where the dark-haired man had placed it, its silver dirk gleaming uppermost. Gently snatched it up, flicked it open. It was entitled: The Chieftain Roll of Glenny. On the first sheet after the title appeared twenty names and

152

addresses together with the 'Knockman', 'Hillman' aliases. Some hundreds, perhaps thousands, more names and addresses were contained in the indexed pages, and these names were entered, not under their own initials, but under those of one or another of the aliases. The book, in effect, was a complete register of Action Group members, chiefs and divisions.

Gently laid the book down open at the list of chiefs, whipped out a notebook, began to scribble. Most of the names were completely unknown to him, but one or two made him round his lips. There were a junior minister, two M.P.s, a shipping magnate, a noted barrister. The one name that didn't figure in the list was the name of the owner of McClune Castle.

The copy complete, Gently tore it from the note-book, folded it, thrust it down his sock. Still through the french doors he could hear the roaring and skidding of the misused Cortina. He picked up the book again, riffled down the index, sprang it open under S. The alias *Strathman* headed the page boldly, followed by a wilderness of Mcs and Macs. He ran his finger down them, turned the page, turned another, and another. To the end of the entry he'd found no address in Strathtudlem, or a village near it. Frowning, he was about to try again when he heard the Cortina's horn sounding urgently. He dropped the book and turned. He was too late. McGuigan sprang panting through the french doors.

At the same moment the inner door opened and the dark-haired man stepped into the room.

'Guard the window, Jamie,' he said, in a low, flat

voice. 'I'm thinking there's something here to be looked into.'

He was a man of Gently's age and a comfortable six feet in height. He was sparely built, with a trace of lankiness, but with strong shoulders and a straight carriage. His hair, seen at closer range, showed flecks and edgings of grey, and his face, which lengthened to a sharp chin, was pale-complexioned and harshly lined. He had a duelling scar on his left cheek. His grey eyes were cold and small.

'So,' he said to Gently. 'You're a common burglar, ma mannie. Stealing in through people's windows – like a true English thief.'

'He's not exactly a burglar, Glenny,' McGuigan growled. 'I ken fine who and what he is – and the lady too, who has been makin' so dooms free with my car.'

'I say he's a burglar,' the dark-haired man said. 'Or else a house-breaker, which is as bad. I catch him here by an open safe while his accomplice creates a diversion outside. You say you ken him. I don't ken him. I ken only the facts before my eyes. I'll just be ringing the police at Logie and committing him to jail."

'Och, no, Glenny!' McGuigan objected. 'You canna be doin' it to such a man.'

'Cannot?' the dark-haired man said, his eyes glittering. 'That's a word I ken nothing about, James o' Knockie. Why cannot I do it?'

'It's just he's no burglar – you couldna make the flea stick. He's the Whitehall mannie I was tellin' you of – he's in with Blayne – he kens all.'

'He does, does he?' the dark-haired man said,

154

flickering a glance at the folio. 'Then what's he doing here, James o' Knockie – who taught him to pry at Castle McClune?'

'I canna say, Glenny.'

'You canna say – but *I* can say, you red-haired loon! He followed you in here.'

'Glenny, I swear—'

'Och, man, be quiet. You're a puling infant.'

McGuigan looked sadly abashed. He stood hanging his head, his ears crimsoned. The dark-haired man looked grimly at Gently, a muscle twitching by the scar on his cheek.

'You're a cunning chiel,' he said. 'No lack of the English guile with you. And here you are, my worst enemy, running free in my own house.'

'Perhaps we could be introduced,' Gently said mildly.

'Ay – my name wasn't in the book! And to think I left it there – plump and plain – instead of locking it away in the safe. You can hold your beard up, James o' Knockie – ye're not the only fule at the fair.'

'I take it you're the Lord Thistle,' Gently said.

'You'll be for taking, like every southron. You're talking to Alan Stewart McClune – McClune of McClune – Lord Inverlochy.'

'Chief Superintendent George Gently,' Gently said.

'And a rare title, that, for a house-breaker.'

'My apologies,' Gently said, 'for irregular entry.'

McClune glared at him. 'You may rue it,' he said. He stood some moments in smouldering silence, his small eyes fixed on the book; then he cast a savage look at McGuigan, who was shifting uneasily in the doorway.

'Back to Knockie, Jamie!' he snapped. 'Or wherever your bit business takes you. I'll handle the English mannie you've brought down on me. Take your car, man – away!'

'Glenny, if I could have a word—'

'Ye heard me tell ye, James o' Knockie!'

McGuigan looked sullen, but drew himself up with stiff dignity and turned to go. At just that moment Brenda walked in.

'Are you leaving us, Jamie?' she inquired coolly. 'Man, it's a peach of a car you have there. I'd be happy to drive it all day long.'

'Miss Merryn—' McGuigan began, from deep in his chest.

Brenda placed a finger on him. 'Don't say it,' she said. 'And let me give you a tip. Radial ply. It'll cut out all that distressing wheel-spin.'

'I would have you know, Miss Merryn—'

'Get out!' McClune bawled. 'No more o' your clatter. If you weren't so susceptible to the sex, Jamie, you'd not have Blayne on your barrow this minute.'

McGuigan breathed fiercely and marched away. McClune listened to the heavy footsteps fading; then he went quietly to the french doors, closed them, came back into the room.

'There goes a great laddie,' he said, 'Jamie McGuigan. You'll scarcely find his better in the glens. But damn it, man, he shouldn't have come havering in here with a London detective on his tail. But this is men's work – I put on the show for him – ye ken I cannot be less than McClune. Miss Merryn (if so they call you), sit ye down. George, ma mannie, take a chair.'

He went across to a Dutch cabinet and poured whisky from a decanter standing on it. He returned with three pot-bellied silver quaighs and handed one to each of them.

'Tae us,' he said. 'George, fine I ken the barrel you have me over. Now down your dram like a douce body, and tell me – in God's name – what you would be after!'

Gently drank the whisky slowly. It had a smooth, dry, heathery quality. He looked at McClune, at the blue-bound folio. McClune had made no attempt to remove it. Gently set down the quaigh.

'I imagine,' he said, 'I'd be after exactly the same thing as McGuigan. He'll have asked you two questions, you'll have given him the answers. I'd like you to do the same for me.'

'Depending,' McClune said. 'Depending, Geordie. What would these two questions be?'

'The first is' – Gently's deceptively mild eyes held McClune's – 'if the killing of Donald Dunglass was ordered by the Nationalist Action Group.'

'Man, man!' McClune exclaimed, slamming his quaigh down with a bang. 'I could stomach such a question from James o' Knockie, who – between ourselves – isn't blessed with much intellect. But to hear it from the likes of you, Geordie, with all your kennings and advantages, is enough to make a man spit and kick his own ancestral furniture.'

'Still, I'm asking it,' Gently said.

'And the answer is no, man. No! The Movement you speak of is a civilized undertaking with no more murder

157

in it than green ginger. We wouldn't soil our hands with violence. Our aims and means are all political. We aren't above twisting the Lion's tail, but there's the limit – we fight clean.'

'I'd like to believe you,' Gently said. 'But that doesn't quite square with what I know of you. We were in Knockie yesterday. We saw militia training. We were held at gun-point and imprisoned.

'I ken – I ken!' McClune exclaimed. 'That fool Jamie told me of it. You accepted satisfaction, he says – it was over-generous – you should have skinned him.'

'But you're not denying you're training militia?'

'Denying it – no. I can't deny it. But the sort of construction you'll maybe put on it – give me your quaigh, man – you're arguing dry.'

He snatched up the three quaighs and refilled them with the excellent whisky. He gave a perfunctory 'Tae us!' and drank his own in two gulps. Then he held his quaigh before his eyes a moment as though appraising its shape and scrolling, before setting it on the table and again turning to Gently.

'Man,' he said. 'Think where ye are – in a wild-like country – with proud men. It's a long, sad, sair story that comes echoin' down from the glens. We're a small nation – some millions of us – with pith and brain but little siller – and no power but our own right to make head against an aggressor. And we're held in tutelage, man. We're the eldest colony of a powerful nation to the south. They make our laws for us, mint our money, station their armed forces in our territory. And it's been goin' on for centuries, man, with bloody oppression and legal, and not a voice raised for us by the tender conscience of other nations. If we were Jews – if we were black – would you daur treat us as you do? If my face was the colour of that ebony chair would you not be thrusting independence on me? But I'm not black – I'm a Scot – I'm one of the race that runs the world – and I must content myself with being a shameful, shabby, second-class English citizen. Will you swallow it, man, being English? Are you proud to have it so with the Scots? Does it make you stand six inches taller because your foot is on our neck? You ken it will come – it must come – when the Land o' the Free is free again – why are you not beside us, helpin' it, pushin' it, clamourin' in the lugs and lobbies of Westminster?'

'I'll be beside you,' Brenda said. 'I'll march up Whitehall with a placard.'

'Ay,' McClune said. 'You're a spirited lassie. I ken that much about ye.'

'This is all very well,' Gently said, 'and I've no axe to grind with the crusade. But training militia is another matter – it comes under the heading of treasonable practices.'

'I'm coming to it,' McClune said. 'But you're only an Englishman, Geordie, and I maun brief you – and by way of preface you'll not mind me saying that "militia" is too strong a term for our outdoor pastimes. You may take my word for it – and whose is better – that the Gorseprick Project is harmless enough, a manner of organized games, you could call it – I wouldn't have given it countenance else. It isn't putting guns in the hands of the ghillies – the ghillies have guns in their hands already. That mannie Dunglass was a fool to kick up about it. There's never a gliff of sinister intent.'

'Not with strong Nationalist feelings behind it?'

'I tell you no, man. You're misconceiving it.'

'And though it results in misconduct towards innocent tourists?'

'Och man, that's explained. Jamie's worried by deer-stealing.'

Gently drank. 'Just the same,' he said. 'My feeling is that military training is going too far. Pinching the Stone of Scone I'd shut my eyes to, but not bullets aimed at my tyres. So I'd rather like your word – and whose is better – that the Gorseprick Project will be cancelled. It would save so much red tape and perhaps unfortunate publicity.'

'Geordie,' McClune said. 'You turn a knife sweetly. You've a surgeonly touch, ma mannie. Maybe I will just be sendin' some lines to a score of names out of yon book. Will it answer the purpose?'

Gently gave a nod. 'To nineteen – as of Friday night.'

'You're a good reckoner, too,' McClune said. 'And I dare not hope you have a poor memory. But touching this other question of Jamie's – I ken we've settled with the first just what were you thinking that would be?'

Gently drank some more. 'You tell me,' he said.

McClune's broad brow wrinkled and he looked askance at his quaigh. 'This is putting me in a queer position, Geordie,' he said. 'It's asking me to point at my own cousins. Murder is an evil thing, that's true, and it behoves a man to help put it down – and if the affair were clear of suspicion I wouldn't hesitate, ye ken. But as it stands it's a cloudy business with cousins squintin' across at cousins – and the McClune looked to guard his own, and not to be communicating his knowledge to police chiefs.'

'The McClune is also the Lord Thistle,' Gently said. 'With the reputation of the Action Group to maintain.'

'True,' McClune said. 'You can press me with that – we'll be under suspicion till the matter is clarified.'

'And one of your cousins is already suspect and in a fair way to being arrested.'

'And as innocent as a babe,' Brenda put in. 'Or are you insinuating Jamie did it?'

'Just listen to the pair of you,' McClune said. 'Will you not leave me a leg to stand on? Was ever a McClune so badgered and mishandled in his own drawing-room in his own castle! Yell have it, will ye?'

'We'll have it,' Brenda said. 'Though all the bens fall into the glens.'

'Which would be a sair catastrophe,' McClune said. 'So I'll say no more – except hand up your quaighs.'

He collected the quaighs and refilled them again. This time he gave the toast standing. The whisky was bringing a flush to his cheeks and his eyes were twinkling down at Gently.

'Our Jamie, you ken – for all I've said – is not without his glimmerings of sense – a man's mind can get strangely clear when his own Craig is nearing the widdie. And he was thinking it was a queerish thing how the murderer kent his movements so well – and the braeside, how the murderer kent that, like maybe it was

161

his own backyard. For one way or another Jamie kens Tudlem almost as well as he kens Knockie, and he couldn't make out in his own mind any Tudlem body he could suspect. And Tudlem, you ken, is fairly remote – it's a few good miles to the next village – and there was no vehicle used that Jamie kent of – but there was the murderer, watchin' and waitin'.'

'Yes,' Gently admitted. 'That puzzled me, though I wasn't in a position to eliminate the villagers. But if it wasn't a villager, who fits? Where did this knowledge-able killer spring from?'

'Aha,' McClune said. 'Ye're no hillman, Geordie, or you wouldn't have puzzled over it long. If the laddie came not from the village and came not down the glen – ask yourself, what's left? He must have come down from the tops.'

'From the tops!' Gently said. 'But there's no path over them.'

'I'm not so damned familiar with them,' McClune said. 'But Jamie tells me there's a way over.'

'But there's nowhere behind them,' Gently said. 'It's just a plateau and peaks running through for miles.'

'You're wrong,' McClune said. 'You must study the map, Geordie. There's a wee glen behind there called Glen Laggart. It runs up high out of Glen Skilling, so you won't find it marked green. But there's good pastures at the top end and a farm they call Snaw-in-June.'

'And – who lives there?'

'Just Jamie's question – who was my tenant at Snaw-in-June. With the additional inquiry, as you well may guess, as to whether that tenant was in the Movement.' He jigged his shoulders. 'For administrative purposes – nothing more nor less, ye ken – we have the Movement divided into sections with a Chief at the head of each.'

'Like communists and anarchists,' Gently said.

'If you put it so – the arrangement is doubtless not original. But that's the way of it, and Jamie had no knowledge of who and who wasna in Dunglass's chiefship.'

'And the answer to that question?'

McClune hesitated. 'This is givin' up my own tenant,' he said. 'Tenant – clansman – honest man – and always punctual with his rent. But I've shown him to you, so I must name him. He's Hector McCracken, of the Bieth McCrackens. He's farmed in Laggart for twenty years and raised a bonnie family on wool and mutton.'

'A member of the Movement?'

'Didn't I say so?'

'An important member?'

'Dunglass's lieutenant.'

'A man of what character?'

'A hanging character,' McClune said. 'A passionate hater of all the English – he and his four blockhead sons. Ay, if there's one who might have scragged Dunglass for cuttin' loose from the Movement it's Hector Bruce McCracken, the wild man of Glen Laggart.'

'And the sons?'

'All of a kidney. Not one of them under six foot two.'

'Would there be a daughter?'

'Ay, such another. She could wrestle evens with her brothers.'

'The original mountain hizzie,' Brenda said. 'She canters around with a socking great dog.'

'That may be,' McClune said. 'There's never a sheep-farm without them – now I mind it, McCracken keeps wolfhounds – my factor, Johnson, was nearly eaten by them.'

'And you gave McGuigan this information,' Gently said. 'What does McGuigan intend to do with it?'

'Not a thing,' McClune said. 'Unless friend Blayne is for running him in. Then he'll come out with it, I doubt not, for all the McGuigans and McCrackens are kin. But man, I hope there'll be a colour put on it that'll keep the Movement on the windy side.'

'Will you talk to McCracken?'

'Will you give me the time?'

They stared at each other. Gently said nothing. McClune solemnly raised his quaigh and tossed back the last of his whisky.

'You're a queer man, Geordie,' he said. 'I can't help liking you, English or not. It's no grief of yours, but you'll be for goin' up Laggart like the Miller o' God on a visit. Am I right?'

Gently gave a faint shrug.

'Ay – you'll be for it, I ken,' McClune said. 'And you must watch your step, Geordie ma mannie, when you're treadin' round Snaw-in-June. But I'll do my best for you – I'll give ye a sayin' – and ye're to forget it, mind, the next day after. If you find you're in trouble up the glen, say: The eagle is flying over Glenny. Have you got it?'

'That's lovely,' Brenda said. 'I'll try to forget it, but that won't be easy.'

'So long as you don't remember it aloud,' McClune said. Och – for me to be giving the Word to southrons!'

CHAPTER ELEVEN

An the Percie cam to Hartshorn Edge
   Wyth his bowmen yn the van,
An he saw the Douglas whytlin a stick
   An bowsin out of a can.

               Chevy Chase (Jedburgh MS)

MCCLUNE ACCOMPANIED THEM across the lawn and bid them farewell at the gate. By the time they arrived back at the Minx he had vanished again into the Castle.

'Do you think he'll be on the phone now,' Brenda said. 'Sending out a May-Day to the clan.'

Gently shook his head. 'I know too much,' he said. 'One glance at that bluebook put me in business. Besides, it's in McClune's interests now to have the matter cleared up promptly. He may not want it pinned on McCracken, but at least that will exonerate the Movement.'

'And of course, you're going to do the Miller of God act – wolfhounds and the kidney notwithstanding?'

Gently started the engine, grinned at her. 'Do you really want me to leave it to Blayne?' he said.

They drove on down, joined the main road, turned west again towards Torlinnhead. Brenda lit a cigarette irritably and glided fierce puffs towards the windscreen.

'Were you planning to drop me off?' she asked.

'That would be sensible,' Gently grunted.

'Oh no it wouldn't,' Brenda said. 'It would be damn silly. Going up there you need someone with you.'

'You forget,' Gently said. 'I've the McClune's protection. Also some experience in handling these matters.'

'And a fat lot of good they're likely to do you when you're about to be eat by ravenous wolfhounds!'

Gently said nothing.

'No,' Brenda said. 'No. If you go you're taking me too, George Gently. At least if I'm with you it will make you more careful, more likely to pull out if things get rough. And I want to go. I'd like to see this ferocious McCracken and his sons. And what's more I decided, when I was driving the Cortina, that I'm more of a heroine than I've been giving out.'

Gently's mouth twitched. 'Perhaps the job doesn't call for a heroine,' he said.

'Well, whatever it calls for I am, so you can consider that settled.'

'If you come, you must do as I say – no questions, no arguments.'

'Oh,' Brenda said. 'That makes it rather harder. But I'm still not letting you go there alone. I don't trust that mountain hizzie an inch – she was playing it coy, but man, she was playing it.'

167

Gently pushed the Minx along. They unravelled Loch Torlinn, passed Kinleary. Excursion traffic dotted the route and was parked suicidally at every viewpoint. At Loch Cray, briefly seen as they threaded a jam at Lochcrayhead, sails blue, white and striped leaned and weaved on slaty water.

'Happy souls,' Brenda observed sourly. 'Little do they know what we're up to. We could use a posse of big brave dinghy-men, padded to the eyes in P.V.C.'

'Oh no we couldn't,' Gently grunted. 'The idea is to give the McCrackens some bait.'

'Perhaps I should strip,' Brenda said.

'Just remember – do what I tell you.'

They came to Skilling and turned down into its mazy spread of trees. The traffic thinned. They passed cottages, reached the lower end of Loch Balva. Here the road divided, continuing on the right its long trek to the head of Skilling, on the left passing below the loch and striking a line to the south of it. They forked left and shortly came to a lefthand junction.

'Check that,' Gently said.

Brenda checked it. It was the back road coming in from Strathtudlem. A mile further on they arrived at a massive divide in the braes southward. A track of the sort now becoming familiar thrust roughly and steeply into this gorge, and a board nailed to an adjacent tree read: *Snow-in-June Farm – Private Road*. Gently parked. He looked at Brenda.

'Here's the battle-plan,' he said. 'We're going in. I'm going to ruffle McCracken, see if I can get him to show his hand. At some stage I may tell you to leave, and

168

you'll leave promptly without arguing. You'll drive to the nearest phone, which is at Skilling village, and ring the police at Balmagussie. Get Blayne, Purdy or whoever and tell them to bring some men up Glen Laggart: explain the situation: if you can't get Blayne, make sure the information is passed to him.'

'Can't we ring Blayne first?' Brenda suggested.

No,' Gently said. '*I may want you to leave*. And I shan't want Blayne coming out here unless I have someone for him to take back. And understand this clearly: it may seem to you I'll be sticking my neck out at some point. Don't let it influence you. Just follow the plan. I'll maybe have an ace up my sleeve.'

'Oh dear,' Brenda said. 'I'm feeling rather less brave than I did an hour ago. You're sure you know what you're doing?'

'Pretty sure,' Gently said. 'And if I find I'm wrong I can still draw my horns in and come quietly back down the glen.'

Brenda shivered. 'Kiss me,' she said.

Gently gathered her close and kissed her.

'Ah,' she said. 'I'm heroic again. Lay on, Macduff – let's go.'

They drove on up Glen Laggart. At first it was little more than a ravine. Rough, craggy cliffs, stained with lichens, carried a slot of sky high above them. The track gnawed and twisted its way upwards with a gloomy cut-off on the left, where white water and green went rumbling down a deep crevasse. Then they came to a waterfall, a thin, shooting, tress-like cascade, and the crevasse closed, the track levelled, the cliffs shallowed, stood farther apart. They were entering a fertile basin in the mountains, a little kingdom hedged by peaks. The braes rose peaceably before, beside them, their lower slopes grazed by sheep. Above the furthest braes lifted a crooked peak with a napkin of white which was not sheep. A pocket of snow, it lay chillily secure in the shadowed, north-facing heights.

Below this peak they began to see the red-painted iron roof of the farm, a low stone building, very bare, with a cluster of outbuildings grouped around it. Sheep-wire enclosed some pens in its neighbourhood. A few stunted firs made a line behind it. Smoke rose from one of the potless chimneys and was the only token of life.

They came closer. Still nobody appeared, though the car must certainly have been visible on the open track.

'Perhaps they are all out,' Brenda muttered hopefully. 'Gone head-hunting or whatever they do on Sabbaths.'

Gently shook his head. 'There's a car in that lean-to. They're probably watching us, getting us figured.'

'Well I wish they wouldn't,' Brenda said. 'And the car's a Skoda. The heathens.'

They entered a fenced yard before the house. Then at last there was movement. In his mirror, Gently saw the tall girl of the crag glide swiftly to the yard-gate, close it, pad-lock it. At the same moment the house door opened and a man stepped out, followed by two wolfhounds. Two other men appeared from behind the house, two more emerged from the outbuildings. They carried rifles. They surrounded the car. The man with the dogs waved his rifle at the car.

170

'Out,' he said, 'ma fine friends. Let's see what the wind has blown in on us. Flora, jist shift a wee out o' my aim – I may be for shootin' your grand English acquaintances.'

'Stay in the car,' Gently told Brenda. He climbed out and walked up to the man with the dogs. The dogs watched him with smoky eyes, planted one each side of their master. He was a man as tall as or taller than McGuigan and of a similar cast of broadboned feature, but he was beardless and his hair was white and his eyes were pale and squinted. His mouth, too, was cruelly thin and pulled into a savage sort of droop, and the long cheeks with trailling furrows gave the face an expression of wildness.

'Hector McCracken?' Gently said.

'Ay,' McCracken said. 'To friend and foe. An' if you come here as the latter, yell rue the day ye set fute in Laggart.'

'I come as a private citizen,' Gently said. 'With the rights of whom you are maybe familiar.'

'I ken them in Scotland,' McCracken said. 'What they'd be in other part I kenna and carena.'

They stood staring at each other. McCracken's rifle lay light and easy in his knobbly hands. His thumb was resting on the safety-catch, his fingers extended along the trigger-guard. The four other men, whose resemblance to McCracken left no doubt of their relation to him, stood holding their rifles in the same way. Only Flora McCracken was unarmed.

'There's been a death in the parish,' Gently said. 'Your neighbour died last Friday night.'

McCracken spat. 'No neighbour o' mine. There's a mountain between us he daredna have climbed.'

'But you dare climb it,' Gently said. 'And I think it likely you often do. It's your short cut to the nearest village – shop, post-office, telephone, bus.'

'I tell you there's no path over there,' McCracken said.

'Ask your daughter,' Gently said. 'She can tell you. She was over there last night, perhaps yesterday afternoon. And if she can get over, so can you.'

McCracken's thumb smoothed the catch back and forth. 'Jist carry on talkin',' he said. 'I'm listenin'. Ye're a bold rash laddie at gi'en words – ma fingers are jerkin' an' jinkin' already.'

'There's a way over the top,' Gently said. 'And you know it. Your sons, your daughter know it too. One or more of you go that way often – like the persons who knew so much about Dunglass's affairs.'

'Is it so, is it so,' McCracken said.

'Yes,' Gently said. 'It is so. And that way went Dunglass's killer, and that way Dunglass's killer returned. Where were you on Friday evening, McCracken?'

'Jist shoot the ugly Englishman, faither!' Flora McCracken cried. 'Put a bullet through his heid an' another through his heart – gie Buska an' Ban a taste o' fresh bluid.'

'Whist,' McCracken said. 'You're too eager. I'm thinkin' tumblin' him ower a crag would suit better. But let's hear more o' his clatterin' yet – let him dig his grave wi' his tongue.'

'Dunglass's killer,' Gently said, 'was a man who knew him, a man Dunglass trusted. A man he thought he could turn his back on when he went with him in the dark. A man he'd known as a comrade. A man who was posing as his friend. A man who nevertheless hated Dunglass so he could strike him down in cold blood. A twisted man. A would-be patriot. A treacherous man. A coward.'

'By jings,' McCracken rasped through his teeth. 'This is more than ma mither's flesh can take – lay haud of him! I'll have his scrapin' tongue out o' his heid.'

'You won't,' Gently said. 'You'll stand your ground and listen, McCracken. Because the eagle is flying over Glenny – *and you're the man who'll have to answer.*'

McCracken's squinted eyes opened stupidly and his hand went slack on the rifle. He stared wildly at Gently, his almost lipless mouth dragging.

'*What* did ye say, Englishman?' he asked.

'Och, let me get at him, faither!' cried Flora McCracken. 'If he kens the Word he's a spy – I'll rend him mysel' – we'll have the dogs on him!'

'Back, lassie!' McCracken said. 'You canna treat the Word i' that fashion.'

'It's stolen, sure!'

'Hauld your clatter! The Word's the Word, an' you canna go over it.'

He let the butt of the rifle fall, his eyes never leaving Gently. It was a signal. Four other rifles sank reluctantly to the ground.

'So,' McCracken said. 'I micht have guessed it from

the way you came whifflin' up to ma door – from your manner o' speakin' to your betters. You wouldna have ventured it on your ain bottom.'

'No,' Gently said. 'I don't usually walk up to a tiger without a gun.'

'Your tongue will ruin you yet,' McCracken said, 'if you wag it for lang enough. What's your business?'

Gently hunched a shoulder. 'The truth,' he said. 'Who killed Dunglass. Why.'

'We ken nothin' of it.'

'You'll have to prove that. The finger is pointing at you, McCracken.'

'Let it point!' McCracken said violently. 'I havena been over the hill this fortnight. On Friday night I was takin' ma ease by ma ain hearthside, in ma ain house.'

'Have you witness to that?'

'Ay, have I. Robbie, tell the Englishman where I was.'

'You were right here, faither,' said one of the young men. 'It's the mortal truth, an' I'll swear to it.'

'Willie?'

'Ay, faither.'

'Wattie?'

'Ay. We were playin' cards till gone twelve.'

'Stevie?'

'Ay. I mind Friday fine.'

'Flora?'

'Ay, faither. We didna shift.'

'So what about that, Englishman?' McCracken said. 'Five credible witnesses sayin' I was here. An' five for each an' every one of us – where will that get ye with a magistrate?'

Gently shook his head. 'It won't work, McCracken. We can prove that one of you was over the hill.'

'Ye canna.'

'Yes. We found fingerprints on the phone that was used to fetch Dunglass out.'

'Fingerprints – phone – I ken nothin'—!'

'The murderer used a Forestry box on the braes. He rang Dunglass and told him his wife was keeping an assignation near the Keekingstane.'

McCracken stared stupidly at Gently. 'He rang Dunglass – tellt him that?'

'Yes.'

'But glory, man – I didna even ken that Mrs Dunglass was lookin' astray!'

'The person who used the Forestry box knew. They knew every detail of those assignations. They knew the place, the man, the road he'd come by, the crag below which he hid his car. They knew a very great deal about it, McCracken. They'd spent a lot of time spying up there. I'd say they were over the top most evenings, going out early, coming in late.'

'Man, I'm runnin' a farm—!'

'Who was it,' Gently said. 'Who was spending their evenings up there on the braes? If it wasn't you you'd know who it was – you do know – and we'll know too, very soon.'

'I'm tellin' you!' McCracken stammered.

'You know who it is. You know their reason.'

'Och!' Flora McCracken cried. 'If you winna shoot him, faither, hand me your gun and leave him to me.'

'Whist, daughter, whist,' McCracken exclaimed.

'Will ye let him outface ye?' the girl cried. 'On your ain sod – your fute on Laggart – an Englishman dingin' you down wi' words? Och, I'm blushin' for you, father. This isna the way o' Hector McCracken. I'll awa' to my kin at Gillieknock, where they carena if the sky is black with eagles.'

'Ye daft bitch!' McCracken snarled. 'Have ye nought in your harps but wildfire? Robbie, take your sister back i' the hoose – I canna think sense wi' her bangin' ma lugs.'

'Ye'll rue it,' she cried. 'Ye'll rue it, McCracken, if you chop mair words wi' the ugly southron.'

'Get her out o' ma sight!' McCracken bawled.

'Come awa', Flo,' said the young man nearest her.

Flora McCracken gave him a fierce look but made no move to obey her father. She stood biting her lips, her brows dragged together, her molten eyes glaring at Gently. McCracken affected not to notice her disobedi-ence.

'So ye have these prints, ye're sayin',' he said to Gently.

'We have them,' Gently said. 'And we'll match them. We'll know who made that call by this evening.'

'But ye canna be sure what the call was about.'

'We don't need to know that when we know who made it. We know it was made at a certain time and that Dunglass went out as a result of it.'

'Ay, but even so,' McCracken said. 'It's not to say the body who made it was likewise the murderer. There's room for argyment there, I'm thinkin', for all you're pretendin' nothin' o' the sort.'

'There's always room for argument,' Gently said. 'But

it's facts and evidence that win convictions. And I've no doubt we'll come by plenty of both when we question the owner of those prints.'

'But if the body who made the call had guid, strong witness – if that body should prove to have been elsewhere – an' there's this other man nearby the spot – it's very argyable he would quarrel wi' Dunglass.'

'Only we happen to know differently,' Gently said. 'And you know differently too, McCracken. Or you wouldn't be poking a gun in my chest and threatening to throw me over a crag.'

McCracken's grim face twisted. 'Ye ken what you're doin', man,' he said. 'But had ye not come here from the quarter ye did, you'd no be traipsin' down Laggart again to be settin' on Blayne. What more do you want?'

'I'd like to see that path.'

'It's more than your puir English feet can tread.'

'I'd still like to see it.'

'Your heid'll no take it. It's for men who've brushed the dew aff the heather.'

'I'll show the cratur' the path, father,' Flora McCracken said unexpectedly. 'If he will see it, he will see it, an' I can show him as well as another.'

McCracken looked at her, his eyes small, then flashed a a quick glance at Gently.

'What d'you say, southron,' he said. 'Will you go up the braes wi' ma daughter?'

Gently hesitated, then shrugged carelessly. 'Why not?' he said. 'She'll know the way.'

'An' your lady-friend too,' Flora McCracken said. 'If we take it slow she'll manage fine.'

Gently hesitated again. 'No,' he said. 'There's the car to get back. Besides, I haven't much time to spare. My friend can go over another day.'

Flora McCracken muttered something, but took a glance from her father and was silent. Gently walked back to the Minx, where Brenda sat pale-faced, eyes scared.

'I'm going over the top,' he said, 'with Miss McCracken. You take the car back to Strathtudlem. I'll see you there in a couple of hours. Have the kettle on for a pot of tea.'

'Are you sure – are you sure?' Brenda faltered. 'I mean, you're not . . . well . . . used to climbing?'

'Oh, I'll be in good hands,' Gently said. 'Never worry about me. Watch your driving.'

Flora McCracken unlocked the gate and Brenda jerkily, clumsily turned the Minx. When she was level with Gently again she halted and wound down her window.

'What are we doing for dinner?' she asked. 'Am I to ring up and book?'

'Of course,' Gently said. 'The sooner the better. Cut along and book two tables.'

Brenda went.

Flora McCracken closed the gate, watched the Minx disappear behind a ridge. She turned, avoiding her father's eye, and stared levelly at Gently.

'I've a sma' business in the hoose,' she said. 'It winna take mair than a minute. So if yell jist bide where you are, I'll be wi' ye – I'll be wi' ye.'

CHAPTER TWELVE

Frankie and Johnny were sweethearts,
  Oh and how they did love.
                    'Frankie and Johnny'

WHILE FLORA MCCRACKEN was gone Hector McCracken stood bearing down on his rifle and scowling stupidly at the ground near Gently's feet. His mouth plucked and twisted and he bored at the earth with the rifle-butt. At last he jerked back his savage grey head and fixed tiny, ice-like eyes on the detective.

'You'll be drawin' the blinkers over me still,' he said. 'I ken it, I ken it. You're a smooth, deceivin' body, like every Englishman that ever breathed. You're a' velvet an' soft speakin' an' innocence an' empty hands, then in a blink the knife's at our craig, an' we dinna ken which way it came.'

'That was much your neighbour's situation,' Gently said. 'With the addition that his back was turned at the time.'

'Dunglass was a traitor, ye weel ken. Back or front, it was no matter wi' him.'

'A subtle distinction,' Gently said. 'But all murderers are traitors. Killing is easy. You stand here alive because other people have honoured their contract.'

'English blethers,' McCracken sneered. 'We ken the value o' rich language. We've had it cuitlin' up our lugs since the days o' Wallace an' the Bruce. But for a' your sophisticatin', Englishman, dinna be weighin' your woo' yet. Ye have your fute where it's fatal for southrons – it's a far call frae the Bow Bells.'

He glowered at Gently, then turned his back. His sons remained staring uncertainly at Gently. One of them, Robbie, had gone to the gate, and leaned massively against it, whistling untunefully.

Flora McCracken returned from the house, her sweater exchanged for a denim jacket. She paused for a moment before her father and looked up steadily into his eyes.

'Shall I send the boys wi' ye?' McCracken muttered.

'What for should I need them?' she replied scornfully.

'Jist watch your step, lassie, wi' yon slimy customer.'

'Dinna fear about that. I ken his like.' She turned to Gently. 'Come, Englishman,' she said. 'Here's an honour you winna have often repeated. You're goin' up the braes wi' McCracken's daughter – I hope you mayna boast about it later.'

'I appreciate that privilege, Miss McCracken,' Gently said.

She looked at him scathingly. 'Perhaps – perhaps no'. But we'll see what you make of a regular hill-path, where the feathers of a' the eagles are black. Let's awa'.'

She set off at a swinging pace towards the firs behind

the house. Gently followed. McCracken, his sons, the dogs stood silently watching them out of sight.

Beyond the firs an easy track followed a contour of the braes and led to a steep rocky gully filled with boulders and rubbish. The route was obviously well-trodden. There was a worn line through the short hill grass. Rocky areas were scratched and abraded and heelmarks were showing in puddles of mud.

Flora McCracken stalked ahead without wasting a back-glance at Gently. She had a springing ease in her step that seemed to mock at the law of gravity. Though so tall, she had the perfect body of some well-developed wild creature, a deer, a snow-leopard. Her footing was rapid but very sure.

They reached the gully. She went straight on up it, never slacking her pace for a moment. Her figure, lean in the jeans and buttoned jacket, went swinging rhythmically away from Gently. Gently let her go. He tackled the gully at his own deliberate pace. When he reached the top, panting and streaming, he found her sitting on a boulder, cool and unblown.

'Is that the best you can do, Englishman,' she sneered. 'I wouldna want to take to the braes wi' you often. I'm thinkin' your roast beef is no' what it was when you were makin' such work at Culloden.'

'I'm out of practice,' Gently said. 'Up here, you can run rings round me, Miss McCracken.'

'Ay, is it comin' to you now?' she said. 'But that should have been thought of before you ventured.'

She sprang off the boulder and marched on, leaving

Gently to wipe his sweat. But now they had climbed on to a heathery top and had a fairly flat section before them. Behind them the Laggart plateau lay partly in view, ahead a range of craggy cliffs. To the right reared the crooked, alp-like peak with its dull, unsunned snow-in-June.

After a while Flora McCracken slowed and permitted Gently to draw abreast of her.

'An' do you feel it quite safe up here, ma man,' she said. 'When your heid is so full o' so many great secrets?'

'Pretty safe,' Gently said. 'That eagle's still flying over Glenny.'

'But Glenny is Glenny,' Flora McCracken said. 'An' there's nought on Laggart Braes but crows. An' Laggart crows are hungry creatures, always ravenin' after carrion.'

'I'll back the eagle,' Gently said. 'I imagine he's used to dealing with crows.'

Flora McCracken stopped, looked carefully all round her. 'I canna get sight of an eagle,' she said.

She kept close to him. They walked on.

'Let me tell you a tale, Englishman,' she said. 'It's about a handsome chiel an' a rich ane, who was for settin' himself up in the hills.'

'Did he come from Glasgow?' Gently asked.

'Ay, from thereabouts,' she said. 'But he was a proper man for a' that, with a dark eye that rinned through ye. An' he was strong, wi' mowin' shoulders an' a neck like a young bull – the lassies were wild for him – he was marrit to a mouse of a female he caredna a rush for.'

'Rich, handsome,' Gently said. 'And a patriot too, I've no doubt.'

'You may weel say so. It was kent an' held o' him he would lead the motion against the southron. He could speak het an' strang, baith at council an' on the stand – he had a voice would sing in your bluid – you couldna withstan' him – you wouldna try. He was elected out o' hand to be leader next to the great chief. He was chief in his own right over the lealest district o' them a'.'

'He had a lieutenant,' Gently said. 'In this very leal district.'

'He had sich a man,' Flora McCracken said, 'as would give his heart's bluid – or take another's.'

'And they were, naturally, often together,' Gently said. 'And this handsome patriot met his lieutenant's family – four hopeful sons with patriotic names, and a fiercely patriotic daughter.'

Dinna scoff at me,' Flora McCracken scowled. 'I winna thole your scornin', Englishman. What if Donnie did cast his een ma way – who so fit as masel' to go beside him?'

'Who indeed.' Gently said. 'My apologies.'

'I didna ken the weakness in him i' those days. I didna ken his heart was false an' fickle – his brain deluded by his anglified upbring. I took him for the man I saw walk in wi' his honour an' loveliness upon him – och, it was that man I loved sae lang, sae true – an' who gied me the same coin. Ma feet didna touch the braes when I went ower the tops to Donnie. I never saw the heather sae fair, never heard the birds sing sae sweet. An' this lang time – it would be three summers, a' goin' by like

183

a dream – was never a cloud came between us – never a harsh word or look. I had it – I had it. It doesna signify where the warld is goin' now.'

They had come to the cliffs and to a second gully, even more steep than the first. Flora McCracken led slowly into it, her eyes staring ahead.

'There were two men,' she said. 'Two Donnie Dunglasses. Ane I loved an' he loved me. Ane is livin' wherever I go, he canna be choked in any grave. Ane is walkin' on the brae-side an' by the burnie an' through the trees. I canna see a windflower blowin' but Donnie is smilin' at me there. There's a sound o' him in the breeze an' a warmth o' him in the sun an' a look o' him in the morn an' a feel o' him in the dark. I couldna have harmed Donnie any mair than harmed masel'. If Donnie were scratched, ma ain flesh would bleed. They say he's deid, but it's a black lie, an' ye may cast it in their teeth – for I'm livin' yet. An' so is ma Donnie.'

She went on climbing, but slackly, allowing Gently to keep pace.

'But what of the other Dunglass,' he panted. 'The one who ran after Poppy Frazers.'

He saw her lithe body jerk. 'So ye ken that, do ye?' she said.

'We know he kept a woman in Balmagussie. A high-class prostitute from Glasgow.'

She hung on a moment. 'Ay,' she said. 'Your English nose would lead you to that. There's a need – there's a need. We're no' so far off it now.'

'When did you find out?' Gently panted.

'What can that matter to you?' she flung back. 'You'll

no be tatlin' about it to Blayne or your southron hizzie wi' her painted chops.'

'I'd say you found out recently – last week.'

'An' if I did – what then?'

'Dunglass had changed. You would have noticed it. You'd have been spying on his movements.'

She climbed a few yards silently. 'Ay, Donnie had changed a' right,' she said. 'He was down in Glesca in May – he wasna the same after that. But I didna spy on him, southron. I wouldn't have spied upon Donnie. I may have guessed – I may have grieved – but I didna go searchin' for his secrets.'

'Who told you, then?'

'There's aye ane to bring the bad news.'

'Your family knew?'

'Ma brothers kent it. I wasna ignorant lang after.'

'What day was this?'

'Jist the Tuesday. Jist the Tuesday after the meetin'. Jist the day Donnie turned a traitor an' a' the truths were comin' out. An' I couldna believe it – an' I was takin' his part – an' Wattie ups an' ca's me a name. An' I askit him what was his meanin' – an' he was ower-gleefu' to tell me. An' I kent . . . I kent . . .'

She hauled herself up to a narrow platform at the top of the gully.

'What was it you knew, Miss McCracken?'

'I kent I'd be killin' that other Donnie.'

She stood waiting for him on the platform, her back pressed against a shaft of rock. They had reached the divide. Beyond the platform was a sheer drop to the

Strathtudlem Braes. It commanded a wide prospect. The strath, the village, the roads leading in and out, the bare tops above the forest, the Lodge, the Stane. Near the shaft where Flora McCracken stood a trough or cleft wore its way down the cliff-face. It looked a desperate sort of thoroughfare, but there was no other to the tops below. Gently climbed cautiously on to the platform.

'Luik, luik,' Flora McCracken said. 'Feast your een on the bonnie outluik, the sweet Glen o' Strathtudlem.'

'It's a good observation point,' Gently said. 'Better than the Stane – it includes the Stane.'

'Does it no',' Flora McCracken said. 'There's little ye canna see from here. An' many's the day I've stood watchin', many the night an' the gloamin' – in the het sun, the dashin' rain, the whirlin' ghosties o' the snaw. I have stood here grey an' stiff but wi' ma heart boundin' like a bird – an' I have stood wi' that same heart bangin' an' burstin' in ma breest.'

'You'd have seen McGuigan's meetings with Mrs Dunglass.'

'Tell me what I wouldna have seen.'

'You knew where he hid his car. You were waiting, watching there – Tuesday, Wednesday, Thursday. Friday.'

'Ay, Friday. An' Friday he came, as I kent he would if I kept ma patience. It was late, late, an' still he sat there, glarin' awa' at his paper. Then he got out an' luiked around, as though he half-kent there was a watcher. Then he jist closed the door quietly an' took the auld path up the braes.'

'Those were your finger-prints on the phone – and on the letter pushed under my door.'

'I warned you, Englishman – you canna say other. But you jist came rushin' on to your fate.'

'You phoned Dunglass. You told him his wife had a lover waiting for her on the braes. You told him to make an excuse to go out, but to double back and to meet you at the Stane.'

'Ay,' she said. 'His legs should have carried him there though his brain kent nothin' o' the affair – it was there we met an' there we loved a thousand an' ane nights together. An' when I saw his dark een – when I heard his voice – I thought I never should get to ma purpose. But he was cauld. His only concern was his reputation an' his pride.'

'McGuigan came.'

'You ken he did. You were sittin' below wi' your London hizzie. He was watchin' you an' watchin' the house, an' the bit o' the track where it comes through the trees. Then you got up an' saw him, which he didna like, an' he pulled back, though he was still watchin' – an' you went aff down, an he went down, an' Donnie's woman jumps into his arms.'

'And Dunglass went to the Stane.'

'Ay. We were hid in those trees you can see. I fetchit Donnie to the Stane an' bid him watch what would happen. An' he sees a', an' it was bitter to him, an' I ken he would have slain them baith. But he didna, he didna, for ma ain dirk was goin' into his back.'

Her hand had been resting under the jacket. Now she suddenly snatched it out. It was grasping a short dagger with a wedge-shaped blade, a blade japanned with dark stains. Her eyes glittered at Gently. She raised the dagger. 'Ma ain dirk, Englishman,' she said. 'Wi' the bluid o' ane traitor glimmerin' on it – an' about to mix wi' that of another.'

'Put your weapon down, Miss McCracken,' Gently said.

'Too late!' she cried. 'You didna lack for a warnin'. But you wouldna be warned, wouldna be told – you would have it. An' here it comes!'

She sprang at Gently with such suddenness that he had barely time to strike down the blow, while the force of the assault threw him back on the rocks. She went down with him. He lay precariously with his head over the edge, grappling for her wrist with one hand, jabbing at her face with the other. But her strength and ferocity were amazing. Her fingers buried in his throat. With a series of sharp, violent snatches she freed her wrist from his grasp. Then the dirk glinted dully above him and he tensed his arm for a desperate parry; but before she could strike something exploded, and the dirk went spinning into the void.

Flora McCracken leapt back with a piercing scream and stood working her fingers and staring wild-eyed. Behind a rockrim, only a few yards distant, McGuigan was leaning with a smoking rifle. She screamed again. She darted past Gently, launched into the gully and disappeared. McGuigan watched her, his rifle pointing, but made no move to interfere.

He cocked a leg over the rim, came sliding down to land on the platform beside Gently. Gently scrambled up. His neck was bleeding and marked with a row of angry bruises. McGuigan looked at them.

'Man,' he said. 'You shouldna go wrestlin' with a wild-cat.'

He blew across the muzzle of the rifle.

'Now all you've got to do is catch her,' he said.

Gently pressed his neck tenderly and looked at the blood on his fingers.

'Thanks,' he said. 'The situation was beginning to get awkward.'

'But are you not surprised, man,' McGuigan said. 'With me poppin' up like an old blackcock – when for all you kent I was takin' my ease in the parlour at Knockie?'

Gently gave him a grin. 'I wasn't surprised,' he said. 'I had you in my mirror from Torlinnhead. If I hadn't thought you were tailing me up here, I might not have pushed the business so far.'

'Och, well,' McGuigan said, his blue eyes abashed. 'I just reckoned on havin' my own back with you – you tailed me fine from Knockie to Glenny – I don't ken yet what way you did it.'

'Professional secret,' Gently said.

'Ay – if that's a term for invisibility. I didn't see *you* in my mirror, man, when I was crossin' the bare tops.'

Gently shrugged, went down on his knees to peer over the airy edge of the platform. Flora McCracken's dirk lay plainly visible on a seam of turf, a hundred feet below.

'I'll fetch it for you,' McGuigan said, also peering. 'It's no' but a scramble down there. An' I'm thinkin' with the bluid on one end, the prints on the other, it doesn't leave Miss Flora with muckle room for manoeuvre. Man, give us your hand. You've lifted an ugly weight off my shoulders – off Mary's too. You'll no lack for friends when your feet are strayin' in this direction.'

He grasped and shook Gently's hand firmly, drawing him close as he did so. Then his eyes began to twinkle and he gave a rumbling chuckle.

'All the same, ma mannie – as I am distant kin o' the McCrackens – there was intermarriage, you ken, about the time o' the Union – an' Miss Flora bein' the spunkie, sonsie lass you have seen – I'm hopin' she leads you a dance through the heather before you clap her into a cell.'

'She'll find Blayne waiting for her below,' Gently said.

'An' waitin' is the word,' McGuigan said. 'You mustn't suppose she'll go trippin' down there an' slap bang into his arms. No, no, man – she's mountain-raised – she'll always keek before she leaps – she'll be away into the back-country, no doubt o' that, an' you will not soon pick up with her there.'

'We can seek her with dogs,' Gently said shortly.

'An' where will that get you?' McGuigan said. 'She'll ken as much about the way o' dogs as the dogs do themselves.'

'We can comb the area with military – use helicopters.'

'Ay, it'll be a grand sight,' McGuigan said. 'But my money'll still be on Miss Flora. This is an uncommon country for gettin' lost in.'

'Then what would you recommend?'

McGuigan's eyes gleamed. 'Och, just Hamish an' one or two o' the laddies. But since they wouldna take orders from you, an' since I'm no' like to give them any, that's just idle clatter. You'll need to be patient, George ma mannie.'

He gave a sudden, wild whoop, thrust his rifle at Gently, then went leaping down the descending cleft with a recklessness that made Gently shudder. At the level of the seam he paused briefly, made a quick, shuffling traverse. He picked up the dirk by its tip. He looked up at Gently, whooped again.

The Minx and two police cars were standing before the farm. Blayne, Purdy and six uniform men were deployed about the yard. When Gently and McGuigan came out of the trees Blayne went loping over to meet them, but it was McCracken, fierce as a bear, who rushed up to reach them first.

'Where's ma daughter – what have you done wi' her?'

He thrust his grim face at Gently's. His grey eyes were wide with hate and his huge fingers curled like hooks. McGuigan tapped him on the shoulder.

'Just stand aside a wee, cousin,' he said. 'Ye're talkin' to a man worth half a dozen o' you – an' a friend o' Knockie's to boot.'

'Where's ma daughter!' McCracken snarled, striking McGuigan's hand aside. 'If you've harmed a finger o' her I'll rend ye apart – where's ma daughter – where's Flora?'

'Now you're bein' less than civil, cousin,' McGuigan said, giving McCracken a poke that sent him staggering.

'An' it does not become a kinsman o' mine who may be standin' upright by my grace an' favour.'

'If ye touch me again I'll kill ye!' McCracken snapped.

'I'll run the risk of it,' McGuigan said. 'An' on that subject, cousin, I'll have you know you were as near dying as breathing yourself, but two hours earlier. I had a bead on your forehead, man, while you were waggin' your gun at the Superintendent, an' had ye made one move the more I would have split your head like a rotten orange.'

'Ye did – ye did!' McCracken spluttered. 'I shallna forget that either, Knockie – but ma daughter – where's ma daughter. If she's harmed, I'll murder ye a'!'

'Your daughter is safe,' Gently said. 'Perhaps you can tell us where to look for her.'

'Ahem – ahem,' Blayne's dry cough interrupted. 'I was just about to put the very same question.'

McCracken stared from one to another of them and a look of cunning came into his eyes. 'So she's awa'!' he said. 'That's the news I wanted – awa', an' the likes o' you dinna ken where. Bring out your constables, Inspector Blayne – bring out your rampin' big doggies – the scent's het, man – set 'em on – but you'll scarcely come by a glisk o' Flora.'

'That may be,' Blayne said. 'But I'm nabbin' you for one, McCracken. I'm thinkin' our chances will be that much better wi' you kickin' your heels in a cell.'

'You canna hold me – you can prove nothin'.'

'I can prove threatenin' behaviour for a start. An' unless I'm much mistaken, I can come up with other charges after a wee crack wi' the Superintendent. No, Hector ma man, your foot's in the bog, an' it won't come out for stainpin' an' rantin'. An' we'll have that wild lassie o' yours too, if not with dogs, then with starvation.'

McCracken spat. 'You'll never find Flora.'

'That's a big word, never,' Blayne said. 'Will I be puttin' the shackles on those outsize wrists, or will you wait douce an' quiet in a car?'

'He'll wait douce an' quiet,' McGuigan said. 'You have the word of his kinsman.'

McCracken gave McGuigan a blazing look, then turned and stumped away towards the cars.

'Well, now,' Blayne said to Gently. 'I ken you're a gliff ahead o' me, man. An' if you're for puttin' me out o' my ignorance, I'm for just sich a charitable motion myself.'

CHAPTER THIRTEEN

This story has no moral,
This story has no end.

'Frankie and Johnny'

GENTLY TALKED. IN a few words he described his
reception by the McCrackens, Flora McCracken's
confession, her violence and flight. What he did not
describe was his tailing of McGuigan and the interview
at Glenny, for which notable exclusion he received
relieved looks from the anxious laird. But Blayne could
not be satisfied so easily.

'And what brought you to Laggart, man?' he asked
flatly. 'It's the neb an' forefront o' the whole interlude
– an' I have an interest in it I'll speak of later.'

'It was his evil genius brought him,' said Brenda, who
had joined them in time to hear Gently's account. 'That,
and his general profligate character. He can never leave
the lassies alone.'

'Ay,' Blayne said, giving Gently a shrewd look. 'I
recall what you were tellin' me, Miss Merryn – that he

met the female McCracken last night, an' there was a passage o' words between them. But I'd not have thought – I haven't heard – she is a very come-hithersome manner o' lassie, an' I'd not have supposed the Superintendent would be so dooms quick off the mark wi' her.'

'Ah, you don't know him, Inspector,' Brenda said. 'There's a ravening wolf under all that phlegm. And the women fall for it. They adore a suave, polite brute like George.'

'But the lassie herself,' Blayne said. 'She gave him small encouragement, by your account of it.'

'Wrong again, Inspector. The lassie knew well enough how to lead him on.'

'Well – howsoever,' Blayne said. 'It would be a rash, inconsiderin' action to come chasin' up here – an' I'm still left wonderin' how it just happened that Flora McCracken was the one we sought.'

Gently hunched his shoulders. 'It's simple,' he said. 'McGuigan and I conferred together. McGuigan had the idea the murderer came from this side. So we just played it along for what it was worth.'

'So that was the way of it,' Blayne said sombrely. 'I could have wished you'd passed your ideas to me, Mr McGuigan.'

'I hadn't the chance,' McGuigan said, thrusting his beard out. 'You were too busy bangin' me wi' questions, man.'

'Aweel,' Blayne sighed. 'It may be so. I ken I was playin' my hand with a flourish – an' the de'il of it is I was findin' my own way – I was near to drawin' up wi' McCracken myself.'

'How was that?' Gently said.

'Och, by listenin' to gossip. A word in my lug from Mattie Robertson. She's an observant woman, as you likely ken – there's not much in Tudlem she doesn't hear tell of. An' she was just mentionin' that McMorris let drop – he's the Forestry ranger who found Dunglass – that the McCracken lassie was aye strollin' the braes, an' once he'd seen her talkin' wi' Donnie.'

'She didn't have much luck, did she?' Brenda said. 'And nobody told her to wear gloves.'

'Ay – I was puttin' it together in my heid,' Blayne said. 'An' addin' Poppy Frazer to the heap, who Dunglass lately fetched from Glasgow. But that's all under the bridge now – it's just to let ye ken I was thereabout – an' for the rest, I'm mighty glad it wasn't maself who took a twirl in the hills wi' Flora McCracken.'

'It was the short way,' Gently said. 'A confession was what we most needed.'

'Short or lang,' Blayne said. 'It would have been no way for me. I ken my limitations, man – I have somethin' more o' patience an' less o' gunpowder. The sort o' work you were makin' today is beyond the talents o' Alistair Blayne.'

Please,' Brenda said. 'Don't butter him up. His conceit is fabulous already.'

'What's worryin' me now,' Blayne said, 'is how we can get him official credit for it.'

'That's easy,' Gently said hastily. 'You won't. I want my name kept out of this. I'm on vacation. I shan't be very pleased if you sick a load of reporters on me.'

'But we'll need your evidence, man—'

'No. The prints, the blood tell their own story. When you catch Miss McCracken you've a confession to face her with. You shouldn't need to bring me in at all.'

Blayne raised and dropped his hands. 'It's against my wishes, ye ken,' he said slowly. 'But if so you'll have it, so it will be – an' with a gratefu' heart from Inspector Blayne.'

They took McGuigan with them down the track to recover his Cortina. He sat in front with Gently, saying nothing till they halted at the spot where he'd left his car. Then he turned to them, his beard lifting, his surprising eyes shyly earnest.

'Man,' he said. 'This is no small matter – we canna brush it off so lightly. I'd like it ill if you left the country without another visit to Knockie. And I ken Mary will want to thank you – and Glenny'll want another crack – and well – it would just be highly convenient if you would consider spendin' a day at the Lodge.'

'Will the trout and venison be on?' Brenda asked.

'Och, will it not, Miss Merryn. And we'll have the pipes – if you're fond o' music – Hamish McTurk is a rare piper. An' we'll give the house a bit of a trim up – an' you'll be bringin' your friends with you – an' I'll ask one or two o' my own – an' there'll be dancin' – och, what do you say?'

'Try holding me back,' Brenda said. 'And that of course goes for George, Geoffrey and Bridget.'

'Keep to that,' McGuigan said, catching her hand. 'Man, they'll hear the noise of us in Stirling. Shall we say Friday o' this week.'

'The obvious and perfect day,' Brenda said.

'Then all's settled – Friday sure – an' come for breakfast if ye will!'

They drove back with the Cortina following them, and saw it turn across the bridge at Strathtudlem. Geoffrey and Bridget were still out and the cottage was heavy with its cool silence. They sat down on the very hard settee. Brenda snuggled into Gently's arms.

'Hold me tight for a little while,' she said. 'Because the certain fact is I'm proved chicken.'

'You're you,' Gently said. 'That's what's important. Who else would you like to be?'

'No one – now,' she sighed contentedly. 'But I'm a hopeless craven, if you did but know. And you must admire girls like Flora McCracken, who can knock you down and nearly knife you. She's the real stuff of heroics. For a Joan McArc, apply to Flora.'

'Hush,' Gently said. 'Who wants a heroine?'

'You, probably,' Brenda said. 'But I'm what you've got, George Gently, so you'll just have to make the best of me.'

'I'll try to resign myself,' Gently said.

'You'd better, you brute,' Brenda said. 'Because I'll never, never let you go up the braes again with a strange woman. You hear me telling you?'

'I hear you,' Gently said.

'Then kiss me – kiss me – and kiss me again.'

Gently kissed her.

Some time after, sooner or later, the others returned.

And that fortnight passed with its suns and its rains and its picnics and expeditions, and they visited Knockie and ate trout and venison and danced and sang in a mild evening; and the morning came when they said goodbye and turned the Hawk, the Sceptre southwards, and Mrs McFie counted her winnings and swore the Major kent who to draw up with.

And still there was no news of Flora McCracken. But it wasn't the end of the story, either.

One hot afternoon in August Gently reported in from a case in the country. He was hungry, tired and in an irritable state from having had to drive through rush-hour traffic. In his outer office he met Inspector Dutt.

'Someone's waiting to see you, Chief,' Dutt said.

'Who?' Gently snapped.

'A woman – I think. She's been in and out of the tank all afternoon.'

'Name?'

'Doesn't give one.'

'Seen her before?'

Dutt shook his head.

'So,' Gently said, 'sling her out. I wouldn't want her to miss her tea.'

But on his way down he glanced into the tank, as the windowless waiting-room was called, and Dutt's stranger was still sitting there. Only Gently knew her. Flora McCracken.

Gently faded back to his office.

'The woman in the tank,' he said to Dutt. 'Get four of the toughest policewomen you can find, have them search her, bring her to me.'

'You know her, then, Chief,' Dutt said.

'Yes,' Gently said. 'Very much I know her. What they'll be searching for is a knife, and they'd better not waste any time finding it.'

Twenty minutes later she was dragged into the office with everyone looking the worse for wear. She'd had a knife. When she saw Gently she set up a screaming that made their ears ring.

'Lock her up!' Gently bawled. 'And someone keep observation on her.'

They dragged her out again. Gently picked up the phone, put through a call to Balmagussie. He doodled on his pad, grinning to himself, thinking how he was going to surprise Blayne. He got Blayne.

'Inspector Blayne? This is Chief Superintendent Gently.'

'Och – my stars! – is it you, Superintendent? An' have you just rang up to congratulate me?'

'Congratulate you – what for?'

'Why, for tyin' up yon case, man – for gettin' a confession oot of Hector McCracken – have you no seen the *Scotsman* this morning?'

Gently took a deep breath. 'No,' he said. 'I haven't seen the *Scotsman* this morning. But I've had Flora McCracken come hunting me with a knife, and she's sitting in a cell here waiting collection.'

'Guidness gracious – are you all right, man?'

'I'm all right. What about this confession?'

'It's just that he made it – and it's very circumstantial – an' jings! – what else could I do but charge him?'

'So?'

Pause at Blayne's end.

'Man, this is awkward,' he said at last. 'I'll fetch the lassie, no fear o' that, but the de'il kens what I'm goin' to do with her.'

'Her confession was also circumstantial.'

'I ken – I ken. An' there's the prints.'

'You can hold her on attempted g.b.h.'

'I can that . . . but what next?'

Another pause.

'I'm thinkin',' Blayne said. 'It's as clear as day that one o' them did it.'

'Clear as day,' Gently said. 'Either Hector McCracken or his daughter.'

'And I'm thinkin' further – and you'll ken the truth of it – that the McCrackens are a chancy clan, and that whichever one finishes up in the tolbooth, there'll be a manner o' justice in it.'

'Something of that sort,' Gently said.

'A manner o' justice,' Blayne said. 'Which should be the guidin' light of all polismen faced with unusual situations. So we'll just fetch the lassie up here – we'll see who suits the bonnet best – and one way or t' ither, we canna go very far astray.'

A week later he rang Gently. His choice had fallen on Flora. She was convicted. She was found of unsound mind. She didn't finish up in the tolbooth.

Note: In selecting mottoes for the chapters I have had occasional recourse to collections laid under contribution by a distinguished predecessor.